THE

LARGESSE OF THE

SEA MAIDEN

THE
LARGESSE
OF THE SEA
MAIDEN

stories by

DENIS
JOHNSON

RANDOM HOUSE
New York

Published in the United States by Random House, an imprint and division of Penguin Random House LLC, New York.

RANDOM HOUSE and the HOUSE colophon are registered trademarks of Penguin Random House LLC.

"The Largesse of the Sea Maiden" was originally published in *The New Yorker.* "The Starlight on Idaho" was originally published in different form in *Playboy.*

Library of Congress Cataloging-in-Publication Data
Names: Johnson, Denis, author.
Title: The largesse of the sea maiden : stories / Denis Johnson.
Description: First edition. | New York : Random House, [2018]
Identifiers: LCCN 2017027298 | ISBN 9780812988635 |
ISBN 9780812988642 (ebook)
Classification: LCC PS3560.O3745 A6 2018 | DDC 813/.54—
dc23 LC record available at lccn.loc.gov/2017027298

Printed in the United States of America on acid-free paper

randomhousebooks.com

2 4 6 8 9 7 5 3 1

First Edition

Designed by Debbie Glasserman

JOE,
CARTER,
WINKY,
BOBBY Z.

CONTENTS

～～～

THE

LARGESSE OF THE

SEA MAIDEN

～～～

SILENCES

After dinner, nobody went home right away. I think we'd enjoyed the meal so much we hoped Elaine would serve us the whole thing all over again. These were people we've gotten to know a little from Elaine's volunteer work— nobody from my work, nobody from the ad agency. We sat around in the living room describing the loudest sounds we'd ever heard. One said it was his wife's voice when she told him she didn't love him anymore and wanted a divorce. Another recalled the pounding of his heart when he suffered a coronary. Tia Jones had become a grandmother at the age of thirty-seven and hoped never again to hear anything so loud as her granddaughter crying in her sixteen-year-old daughter's arms. Her husband Ralph said it hurt his ears whenever his brother opened his mouth in public, because his brother had Tourette syndrome and erupted with remarks like "I masturbate! Your penis smells good!" in front of perfect strangers on a bus, or during a movie, or even in church.

Young Chris Case reversed the direction and introduced the topic of silences. He said the most silent thing he'd ever heard was the land mine taking off his right leg outside Kabul, Afghanistan.

As for other silences, nobody contributed. In fact, there came a silence now. Some of us hadn't realized that Chris had lost a leg. He limped, but only slightly. I didn't even know he'd fought in Afghanistan. "A land mine?" I said.

"Yes, sir. A land mine."

"Can we see it?" Deirdre said.

"No, ma'am," Chris said. "I don't carry land mines around on my person."

"No! I mean your leg."

"It was blown off."

"I mean the part that's still there!"

"I'll show you," he said, "if you kiss it."

Shocked laughter. We started talking about the most ridiculous things we'd ever kissed. Nothing of interest. We'd all kissed only people, and only in the usual places. "All right, then," Chris told Deirdre, "here's your chance for the conversation's most unique entry."

"No, I don't want to kiss your leg!"

Although none of us showed it, I think we all felt a little irritated with Deirdre. We all wanted to see.

Morton Sands was there too that night, and for the most part he'd managed to keep quiet. Now he said, "Jesus Christ, Deirdre."

"Oh, well. Okay," she said.

Chris pulled up his right pant leg, bunching the cuff about halfway up his thigh, and detached his prosthesis, a device of chromium bars and plastic belts strapped to his knee, which was intact and swiveled upward horribly to present the puckered end of his leg. Deirdre got down on her bare knees before him, and he hitched forward in his seat—the couch, Ralph Jones was sitting beside him—to move the scarred stump within two inches of Deirdre's face. Now she started to cry. Now we were all embarrassed, a little ashamed.

For nearly a minute, we waited.

Then Ralph Jones said, "Chris, I remember when I saw you fight two guys at once outside the Aces Tavern. No kidding," Jones told the rest of us, "he went outside with these two guys and beat the crap out of both of them."

"I guess I could've given them a break," Chris said. "They were both pretty drunk."

"Chris, you sure kicked some ass that night."

In the pocket of my shirt I had a wonderful Cuban cigar. I wanted to step outside with it. The dinner had been one of our best, and I wanted to top off the experience with a satisfying smoke. But you want to see how this sort of thing turns out. How often will you witness a woman kissing an amputation? Jones, however, had ruined everything by talking. He'd broken the spell. Chris worked the prosthesis back into place and tightened the straps and rearranged his pant leg. Deirdre stood up and wiped her eyes and smoothed her skirt and took her seat, and that was that. The outcome of all this was that Chris and Deirdre, about six months later, down at the courthouse, in the presence of very nearly the same group of friends, were married by a magistrate. Yes, they're husband and wife. You and I know what goes on.

ACCOMPLICES

Another silence comes to mind. A couple of years ago Elaine and I had dinner at the home of Miller Thomas, formerly the head of my agency in Manhattan. Right—he and his wife Francesca ended up out here too, but considerably later than Elaine and I—once my boss, now a San Diego retiree. We finished two bottles of wine with dinner, maybe three bottles. After dinner we had brandy. Before dinner we had cocktails. We didn't know each other particularly well, and maybe we used the liquor to rush past that fact. After the brandy I started drinking scotch, and Miller drank bourbon, and, although the weather was warm enough that the central air conditioner was running, he pronounced it a cold night and lit a fire in his fireplace. It took only a squirt of fluid and the pop of a match to get an armload of sticks crackling and blazing, and then he laid on a couple of large chunks he said were good, seasoned oak. "The capitalist at his forge," Francesca said.

At one point we were standing in the light of the flames, I and Miller Thomas, seeing how many books each man could balance on his outflung arms, Elaine and Francesca loading them onto our hands in a test of equilibrium which both of us failed repeatedly. It became a test of strength. I don't know who won. We called for more and more books, and our women piled them on until most of Miller's library lay around us on the floor. He had a small Marsden Hartley canvas mounted above the mantel, a crazy, mostly blue landscape done in oil, and I said that perhaps that wasn't the place for a painting like this one, so near the smoke and heat, such an expensive painting. And the painting was masterly, too, from what I could see of it by dim lamps and firelight, amid books scattered all over the floor . . . Miller took offense. He said he'd paid for this masterpiece, he owned it, he could put it where it suited him. He moved very near the flames and took down the painting and turned to us holding it before him and declared that he could even, if he wanted, throw it in the fire and leave it there. "Is it art? Sure. But listen," he said, "art doesn't own it. My name ain't Art." He held the canvas flat like a tray, landscape up, and tempted the flames with it, thrusting it in and out . . . And the strange thing is that I'd heard a nearly identical story about Miller Thomas and his beloved Hartley landscape some years before, about an evening very similar to this one, the drinks and wine and brandy and more drinks, the rowdy conversation, the scattering of books, and finally Miller thrusting this painting toward the flames and calling it his own property and threatening to burn it. On that previous night his guests had talked him down from the heights, and he'd hung the painting back in its place, but on our night—why?—none of us found a way to object as he added his property to the fuel and turned his back and walked away. A black spot appeared on the canvas and spread out in a sort of smoking puddle that gave rise to tiny flames. Miller sat in a chair across the living room, by the flickering window, and observed from that distance with a drink in his hand. Not a word, not a move, from any of us. The wooden frame popped marvelously in the silence while the great painting cooked away, first black and twisted, soon gray and fluttering, and then the fire had it all.

AD MAN

This morning I was assailed by such sadness at the velocity of life—the distance I've traveled from my own youth, the persistence of the old regrets, the new regrets, the ability of failure to freshen itself in novel forms—that I almost crashed the car. Getting out at the place where I do the job

I don't feel I'm very good at, I grabbed my briefcase too roughly and dumped half of its contents in my lap and half in the parking lot, and while gathering it all up I left my keys on the seat and locked the car manually—an old man's habit—and trapped them in the RAV.

In the office, I asked Shylene to call a locksmith and then get me an appointment with my back-man.

In the upper right quadrant of my back I have a nerve that once in a while gets pinched. The T4 nerve. These nerves aren't frail little ink lines; they're cords as thick as your pinky finger. This one gets caught between tense muscles, and for days, even for weeks, there's not much to be done but take aspirins and get massages and visit the chiropractor. Down my right arm I feel a tingling, a numbness, sometimes a dull, sort of muffled torment, or else a shapeless, confusing pain.

It's a signal: It happens when I'm anxious about something.

To my surprise, Shylene knew all about this something. Apparently she finds time to be Googling her bosses, and she'd learned of an award I was about to receive in, of all places, New York—for an animated television commercial. The award goes to my old New York team, but I was the only one of us attending the ceremony, possibly the only one interested, so many years down the line. This little gesture of acknowledgment put the finishing touches on a depressing picture. The people on my team had gone on to other teams, fancier agencies, higher accomplishments. All I'd done in better than two decades was to tread forward until I reached the limit of certain assumptions, and step off. Meanwhile, Shylene was oohing, gushing, like a proud nurse who expects you to marvel at all the unholy procedures the hospital has in store for you. I said to her, "Thanks, thanks."

When I entered the reception area, and throughout this transaction, Shylene wore a flashy sequined carnival masque. I didn't ask why.

Our office environment is part of the new wave. The whole agency works under one gigantic big top like a circus—not crowded, quite congenial, all of it surrounding a spacious break-time area with pinball machines and a basketball hoop, and every Friday during the summer months we have a Happy Hour with free beer from a keg.

In New York I made commercials. In San Diego I write and design glossy brochures, mostly for a group of western resorts where golf is played and horses take you along bridle paths. Don't get me wrong—California's full of beautiful spots; it's a pleasure to bring them to the attention of people who might enjoy them. Just, please, not with a badly pinched nerve.

When I can't stand it I take the day off and visit the big art museum in Balboa Park. Today, after the locksmith got me back in my car, I drove to the museum and sat in on part of a lecture in one of its side-rooms, a woman Outsider artist raving, "Art is man and man is art!" I listened for five minutes, and what little of it she managed to make comprehensible didn't even merit being called shallow. Just the same, her paintings were slyly designed, intricately patterned, and coherent. I wandered from wall to wall, taking some of it in, not much. But looking at art for an hour or so always changes the way I see things afterward—this day, for instance, a group of mentally handicapped adults on a tour of the place with their twisted, hovering hands and cocked heads, moving among the works like cheap cinema zombies, but good zombies, zombies with minds and souls and things to keep them interested. And outside, where they normally have a lot of large metal sculptures, the grounds were being dug up and reconstructed—a dragline shovel nosing the rubble monstrously, and a woman and child watching, motionless, the little boy standing on a bench with his smile and sideways eyes and his mother beside him, holding his hand, both so still, like a photograph of American ruin.

Next I had a session with a chiropractor dressed up as an elf.

It seemed the entire staff at the medical complex near my house were costumed for Halloween, and while I waited out front in the car for my appointment, the earliest one I could get that day, I saw a Swiss milkmaid coming back from lunch, then a witch with a green face, then a sunburst-orange superhero. Then I had the session with the chiropractor in his tights and drooping cap.

As for me? My usual guise. The masquerade continues.

FAREWELL

Elaine got a wall phone for the kitchen, a sleek blue one that wears its receiver like a hat, with a caller ID readout on its face just below the keypad. While I eyeballed this instrument, having just come in from my visit with the chiropractor, a brisk, modest tone began, and the tiny screen showed ten digits I didn't recognize. My inclination was to scorn it like any other unknown. But this was the first call, the inaugural message.

As soon as I touched the receiver I wondered if I'd regret this, if I was holding a mistake in my hand, if I was pulling this mistake to my head and saying "Hello" to it.

The caller was my first wife, Virginia, or Ginny, as I'd always called her. We'd been married long ago, in our early twenties, and put a stop to it after three crazy years. Since then we hadn't spoken, we'd had no reason to, but now we had one. Ginny was dying.

Her voice came faintly. She told me the doctors had closed the book on her, she'd ordered her affairs, the good people from hospice were in attendance.

Before she ended this earthly transit, as she called it, Ginny wanted to shed any kind of bitterness against certain people, certain men, especially me. She said how much she'd been hurt, and how badly she wanted to forgive me, but she didn't know whether she could or not—she hoped she could—and I assured her, from the abyss of a broken heart, that I hoped so too, that I hated my infidelities and my lies about the money, and the way I'd kept my boredom secret, and my secrets in general, and Ginny and I talked, after forty years of silence, about the many other ways I'd stolen her right to the truth.

In the middle of this I began wondering, most uncomfortably, in fact with a dizzy, sweating anxiety, if I'd made a mistake—if this wasn't my first wife Ginny, no, but rather my second wife, Jennifer, often called Jenny. Because of the weakness of her voice and my own humming shock at the news, also the situation around her as she tried to speak to me on this very important occasion—folks coming and going, and the sounds of a respirator, I supposed—now, fifteen minutes into this call, I couldn't remember if she'd actually said her name when I picked up the phone and I suddenly didn't know which set of crimes I was regretting, wasn't sure if this dying farewell clobbering me to my knees in true repentance beside the kitchen table was Virginia's, or Jennifer's.

"This is hard," I said. "Can I put the phone down a minute?" I heard her say okay.

The house felt empty. "Elaine?" I called. Nothing. I wiped my face with a dishrag and took off my blazer and hung it on a chair and called out Elaine's name one more time and then picked up the receiver again. There was nobody there.

Somewhere inside it, the phone had preserved the caller's number, of course, Ginny's number or Jenny's, but I didn't look for it. We'd had our talk, and Ginny or Jenny, whichever, had recognized herself in my frank apologies, and she'd been satisfied—because, after all, both sets of crimes had been the same.

I was tired. What a day. I called Elaine on her cellphone. We agreed she might as well stay at the Budget Inn on the east side. She volunteered out there teaching adults to read, and once in a while she got caught late and stayed over. Good. I could lock all three locks on the door and call it a day. I didn't mention the previous call. I turned in early.

I dreamed of a wild landscape—elephants, dinosaurs, bat caves, strange natives, and so on.

I woke, couldn't go back to sleep, put on a long terry-cloth robe over my pj's and slipped into my loafers and went walking. People in bathrobes stroll around here at all hours, but not often, I think, without a pet on a leash. Ours is a good neighborhood—a Catholic church and a Mormon one, and a posh townhouse development with much open green space, and on our side of the street some pretty nice smaller homes.

I wonder if you're like me, if you collect and squirrel away in your soul certain odd moments when the Mystery winks at you, when you walk in your bathrobe and tasseled loafers, for instance, well out of your neighborhood and among a lot of closed shops, and you approach your very faint reflection in a window with words above it. The sign said "Sky and Celery."

Closer, it read "Ski and Cyclery."

I headed home.

WIDOW

I was having lunch one day with my friend Tom Ellis, a journalist—just catching up. He said he was writing a two-act drama based on interviews he'd taped while gathering material for an article on the death penalty, two interviews in particular.

First he'd spent an afternoon with a death row inmate in Virginia, the murderer William Donald Mason, a name not at all famous here in California, and I don't know why I remember it. Mason was scheduled to die the next day, twelve years after killing a guard he'd taken hostage during a bank robbery.

Other than his last meal of steak, green beans, and a baked potato, which would be served to him the following noon, Mason knew of no future outcomes to worry about and seemed relaxed and content. Ellis quizzed him about his life before his arrest, his routine there at the prison, his views on the death penalty—Mason was against it—and his opinion as to an afterlife—Mason was for it.

The prisoner talked with admiration about his wife, whom he'd met and married some years after landing on death row. She was the cousin of a fellow inmate. She waited tables in a sports bar—great tips. She liked reading, and she'd introduced her murderer husband to the works of Charles Dickens and Mark Twain and Ernest Hemingway. She was studying for a realtor's license.

Mason had already said goodbye to his wife. The couple had agreed to get it all out of the way a full week ahead of the execution, to spend several happy hours together and part company well out of the shadow of Mason's last day.

Ellis said he'd felt a fierce, unexpected kinship with this man so close to the end because, as Mason himself pointed out, this was the last time Mason would be introduced to a stranger, except for the people who would arrange him on the gurney the next day and set him up for his injection. Tom Ellis was the last new person he'd meet, in other words, who wasn't about to kill him. The next day everything proceeded according to the schedule, and about eighteen hours after Ellis talked with him, William Mason was dead.

A week later Ellis interviewed the new widow, Mrs. Mason, and learned that much of what she'd told her husband was false.

Ellis located her in Norfolk, working not in any kind of sports bar, but instead in a basement sex emporium near the waterfront, in a one-on-one peep show. In order to talk to her Ellis had to pay twenty dollars and descend a narrow stairway lit with purple bulbs and sit in a chair before a curtained window. He was shocked when the curtain vanished upward to reveal the woman already completely nude, sitting on a stool in a padded booth. Then it was her turn to be shocked when Ellis introduced himself as a man who'd shared an hour or two of her husband's last full day on earth. Together they spoke of the prisoner's wishes and dreams, his happiest memories and his childhood grief, the kinds of things a man shares only with his wife. Her face, though severe, was pretty, and she displayed her parts to Tom unselfconsciously, yet without the protection of anonymity. She wept, she laughed, she shouted, she whispered, all of this into a telephone handset she held to her head while her free hand gestured in the air or touched the glass between them.

As for having told so many lies to the man she'd married—that was one of the things she laughed about. She seemed to assume anybody else would have done the same. In addition to her bogus employment and her imaginary studies in real estate, she'd endowed herself with a religious soul and joined the membership of a nonexistent church. Thanks to all her fabrications, William Donald Mason had died a proud and happy husband.

And just as he'd been surprised by a sudden intimacy with the condemned killer, my friend felt very close to the widow because they were talking with each other about life and death while she displayed her nakedness before him, sitting on the stool with her red, spike-heeled pumps planted wide apart on the floor. I asked him if they'd ended up making love, and he said no, but he'd wanted to, he certainly had, and he was convinced the naked widow had felt the same, though you weren't allowed to touch the women in those places, and this dialogue, and for that matter both of them—the death row interview and the interview with the naked widow—had taken place through glass partitions made to withstand any kind of passionate assault.

At the time, the idea of telling her what he wanted had seemed terrible. Now Tom regretted his shyness. In the play, as he described it for me, the second act would end differently.

Before long we wandered into a discussion of the difference between repentance and regret. You repent the things you've done, and regret the chances you let get away. Then, as sometimes happens in a San Diego café—more often than you'd think—we were interrupted by a beautiful young woman selling roses.

ORPHAN

The lunch with Tom Ellis took place a couple of years ago. I don't suppose he ever wrote the play; it was just a notion he was telling me about. It came to mind today because this afternoon I attended the memorial service of an artist friend of mine, a painter named Tony Fido, who once told me about a similar experience.

Tony found a cellphone on the ground near his home in National City, just south of here. He told me about this the last time I saw him, a couple of months before he disappeared, or went out of communication. First he went out of communication, then he was deceased. But when he told me this story there was no hint of any of that.

Tony noticed the cellphone lying under an oleander bush as he walked around his neighborhood. He picked it up and continued his stroll and before long felt it vibrating in his pocket. When he answered, he found himself talking to the wife of the owner—the owner's widow, actually, who explained she'd been calling the number every thirty minutes or so since her husband's death not twenty-four hours before.

Her husband had been killed the previous afternoon in an accident at the intersection where Tony had found the cellphone. An old woman in a Cadillac had run him down. At the moment of impact, the device had been torn from his hand.

The police said they hadn't noticed any phone around the scene. It hadn't been among the belongings she'd collected at the morgue. "I knew he lost it right there," she told Tony, "because he was talking to me at the very second when it happened."

Tony offered to get in his car and deliver the phone to her personally, and she gave him her address in Lemon Grove nine miles distant. When he got there he discovered that the woman was only twenty-two and quite attractive, and that she and her husband had been going through a divorce.

At this point in the telling, I thought I knew where his story was headed.

"She came after me. I told her, 'You're either from Heaven or from Hell.' It turned out she was from Hell."

Whenever he talked, Tony kept his hands moving—grabbing and rearranging small things on the tabletop—while his head rocked from side to side and back and forth. Sometimes he referred to a "force of rhythm" in his paintings. He often spoke of "motion" in the work.

I didn't know much about Tony's background. I can say he was in his late forties but seemed younger. I'd met him at the Balboa Park museum, where he appeared at my shoulder while I looked at an Edward Hopper painting of a Cape Cod gas station. Tony offered his critique, which was lengthy, meticulous, and scathing—and which was focused on technique, only on technique—and spoke of his contempt for all painters, and finished by saying, "I wish Picasso was alive, I'd challenge him—he could do one of mine and I could do one of his."

"You're a painter yourself."

"A better painter than this guy," he said of Edward Hopper.

"Well, whose work would you say is any good?"

"The only painter I admire is God. He's my biggest influence."

We began having coffee together two or three times a month, always, I have to admit, at Tony's initiation. Usually I drove to his lively disheveled Hispanic neighborhood to see him, there in National City. I like primitive art, and I like folk tales, so I enjoyed visiting his rambling old home, where he lived surrounded by his paintings like an orphan king in a cluttered castle.

The house had been in his family since 1939. For a while it was a boardinghouse—a dozen bedrooms, each with its own sink. "Damn place has a jinx or whammy: First Spiro—Spiro watched it till he died. Mom watched it till she died. My sister watched it till she died. Now I'll be here till I die," he said, hosting me shirtless, his hairy torso dabbed all over with paint, talking so fast I could rarely follow. He did seem deranged. But blessed, decidedly so, with a self-deprecating and self-orienting humor the genuinely mad seem to have misplaced. What to make of somebody like that? "Richards, in *The Washington Post*," he once said, "compared me to Melville." I have no idea who Richards was. Or who Spiro was.

Tony never tired of his voluble explanations, his self-exegesis—the works almost coded, as if to fool or distract the unworthy. They weren't the child-drawings of your usual schizophrenic outsider artist, but efforts a little more skillful, on the order of tattoo art, oil on canvases around four by six feet in size, crowded with images but highly organized, all on Biblical themes, mostly dire and apocalyptic, and all with the titles printed neatly right on them. One of his works, for instance—three panels depicting the end of the world and the advent of heaven—was called

"MYSTERY BABYLON MOTHER OF HARLOTS REVE-
LATION 17:1–7."

This period when I was seeing a bit of Tony Fido coincided with an era in the world of my unconscious, an era
when I was troubled by the dreams I had at night. They were
long and epic, detailed and violent and colorful. They ex-
hausted me. I couldn't account for them. The only medica-
tion I took was something to bring down my blood pressure,
and it wasn't new. I made sure I didn't take food just before
going to bed; I avoided sleeping on my back, steered clear of
disturbing novels and TV shows. For a month, maybe six
weeks, I dreaded sleep. Once I dreamed of Tony—I defended
him against an angry mob, keeping the seething throng at
bay with a butcher knife. Often I woke up short of breath,
shaking, my heartbeat rattling my ribs, and I cured my
nerves with a solitary walk, no matter the hour. And once—
maybe the night I dreamed about Tony, I don't remember—I
had the kind of moment or visitation I treasure, when the
flow of life twists and untwists, all in a blink—think of a taut
ribbon flashing: I heard a young man's voice in the parking
lot of the Mormon church in the dark night telling someone,
"I didn't bark. That wasn't me. I didn't bark."

I never found out how things turned out between Tony
and the freshly widowed twenty-two-year-old. I'm pretty
sure it went no farther, and there was no second encounter,

certainly no ongoing affair—because he more than once complained, "I can't find a woman, none, I'm under some kind of a damn spell." He believed in spells and whammies and such, in angels and mermaids, omens, sorcery, windborne voices, in messages and patterns. All through his house were scattered twigs and feathers possessing a mysterious significance, rocks that had spoken to him, stumps of driftwood whose faces he recognized. And in any direction, his canvases like windows opening onto lightning and smoke, ranks of crimson demons and flying angels, gravestones on fire, and scrolls, chalices, torches, swords.

Last week a woman named Rebecca Stamos, somebody I'd never heard of, called me to say our mutual friend Tony Fido was no more. He'd killed himself. As she put it, "He took his life."

For two seconds the phrase meant nothing to me. "Took it," I said . . . Then, "Oh, my goodness."

"Yes, I'm afraid he committed suicide."

"I don't want to know how. Don't tell me how." Honestly, I can't imagine why I said that.

MEMORIAL

A week ago Friday—nine days ago—the eccentric religious painter Tony Fido stopped his car on Interstate 8 about sixty miles east of San Diego, on a bridge above a deep, deep ravine, and climbed over the railing and stepped into the air. He mailed a letter beforehand to Rebecca Stamos, not to explain himself, but only to say goodbye and pass along the phone numbers of some friends.

Sunday I attended Tony's memorial service, for which Rebecca Stamos had reserved the band room of the middle school where she teaches. We sat in a circle with cups and saucers on our laps, in a tiny grove of music stands, and volunteered, one by one, our memories of Tony Fido. There were only five of us: Our hostess Rebecca, plain and stout, in a sleeveless blouse and a skirt that reached down to her white tennis shoes; myself in the raiment of my order, the blue blazer, khaki chinos, tasseled loafers; two middle-aged women of the sort to own a couple of small obnoxious dogs—they called Tony "Anthony"; a chubby young man in a green oversuit—some kind of mechanic—sweating. Tony's neighbors? Family? None.

Only the pair of ladies who'd arrived together actually knew each other. None of the rest of us had ever met before. These were friendships, or acquaintances, that Tony had kept one by one. He'd met us all the same way—he'd materialized beside us at an art museum, an outdoor market, a doctor's waiting room, and he'd begun to talk. I was the only one of us even aware he devoted all his time to painting canvases. The others thought he owned some kind of business—plumbing or exterminating or looking after private swimming pools. One believed he came from Greece, others assumed Mexico, but I'm sure his family was Armenian, long established in San Diego County. Rather than memorializing him, we found ourselves asking, "Who the hell was this guy?"

Rebecca had this much about him: While he was still in his teens, Tony's mother had killed herself. "He mentioned her death more than once," Rebecca said. "It was always on his mind." To the rest of us this came as new information.

Of course it troubled us to learn that his mother had taken her own life too. Had she jumped? Tony hadn't told, and Rebecca hadn't asked.

With little to offer about Tony in the way of biography, I shared some remarks of his that had stuck in my thoughts. "I couldn't get into ritzy art schools," he told me once. "Best thing that ever happened to me. It's dangerous to be taught art." And he said, "On my twenty-sixth birthday, I quit signing my work. Anybody who can paint like that, have at it, and take the credit." He got a kick out of showing me a passage in his hefty black Bible—first book of Samuel, chapter 6?—where the idolatry of the Philistines earns them a plague of hemorrhoids. "Don't tell me God doesn't have a sense of humor."

And another of his insights, one he shared with me several times: "We live in a catastrophic universe—not a universe of gradualism."

That one had always gone right past me. Now it sounded ominous, prophetic. Had I missed a message? A warning?

The man in the green jumpsuit, the garage mechanic, reported that Tony had plunged from our nation's highest concrete-beam bridge down into Pine Valley Creek, a flight of 440 feet. The span, completed in 1974 and named the Nello Irwin Greer Memorial Bridge, was the first in the United States to be built using, according to the mechanic, "the cast-in-place segmental balanced cantilever method." I wrote it down on a memo pad. I can't recall the mechanic's name. His breast-tag said "Ted," but he introduced himself as someone else.

Anne and her friend, whose name also slipped past me— the pair of women—cornered me afterward. They seemed to think I should be the one to take final possession of a three-ring binder full of recipes that Tony had loaned them—the collected recipes of Tony's mother. I determined I would give it to Elaine. She's a wonderful cook, but not as a regular thing, because nobody likes to cook for two. Too much work and too many leftovers. I told them she'd be glad to get the book.

The binder was too big for any of my pockets. I thought of asking for a bag, but I failed to ask. I didn't know what to do with it but carry it home in my hands and deliver it to my wife.

Elaine was sitting at the kitchen table, before her a cup of black coffee and half a sandwich on a plate.

I set the notebook on the table next to her snack. She stared at it. "Oh," she said, "from your painter." She sat me down beside her and we went through the notebook page by page, side by side.

Elaine: She's petite, lithe, quite smart; short gray hair, no makeup. A good companion. At any moment—the very next second—she could be dead.

I want to depict this book carefully, so imagine holding it in your hands, a three-ring binder of bright red plastic weighing about the same as a full dinner plate, and now setting it in front of you on the table. As you open it you find the pink title page, "Recipes. Caesarina Fido," covering a two-inch thickness of white college-ruled three-hole paper, the first inch or so the usual, the casseroles and pies and salad dressings, every aspect of breakfast, lunch, and supper, all written with a blue ballpoint. Halfway through the collection, Tony's mother introduces ink in many colors, mostly green, red, and purple, but also pink, and a yellow somewhat hard to make out; and as these colors come along her penmanship enters a kind of havoc, the letters swell and shrink, several pages big and loopy, leaning to the right, and then for the next many pages leaning to the left, then back the other way; and here, where these wars and changes begin, and for better than a hundred pages, all the way to the last page, the recipes are only for cocktails. Every kind of cocktail.

Earlier that afternoon, as Anne handed the binder over to me at Tony's memorial, she made a curious remark. "Anthony spoke very highly of you. He said you were his best friend." I thought it was a joke, but Anne meant this seriously.

Tony's best friend? I was confused. I'm still confused. I hardly knew him.

CASANOVA

When I returned to New York City to pick up my prize at The American Advertisers Awards, I'm not sure I expected to enjoy myself. But on the second day, killing time before the ceremony, walking north through midtown in my dark ceremonial suit and trench coat, skirting the park, strolling south again, feeling the pulse and listening to the traffic noise rising among high buildings, I had a homecoming. The day was sunny, fine for walking, brisk, and getting brisker—and in fact, as I cut a diagonal through a little plaza somewhere above Fortieth Street, the last autumn leaves leapt up from the pavement and swirled around our heads, and a sudden misty quality in the atmosphere above seemed to solidify into a ceiling both dark and luminous, and the passersby hunched into their collars, and two minutes later the gusts had settled into a wind, not hard, but steady and cold, and my hands dove into my coat pockets. A bit of rain speckled the pavement. Random snowflakes spiraled in the air. All around me, people seemed to be evacuating the scene, while across the square a vendor shouted that he was closing his cart and you could have his wares for practically nothing, and for no reason I could have named I bought two of his rat-dogs with everything and a cup of doubtful coffee and then learned the reason—they were wonderful. I nearly ate the napkin. New York!

Once I lived here. Went to Columbia University, studying history first, then broadcast journalism. Worked for a couple of pointless years at the *Post*, and then for thirteen tough but prosperous years at Castle and Forbes on Fifty-Fourth, just off Madison Avenue. And then took my insomnia, my afternoon headaches, my doubts and my antacid tablets to San Diego and lost them in the Pacific Ocean. New York and I didn't quite fit. I knew it the whole time. Some of my Columbia classmates came from faraway places like Iowa and Nevada, as I had come a shorter way from New Hampshire, and after graduation they'd been absorbed into Manhattan and had lived here ever since. I didn't last. I always say, "It was never my town."

Today it was all mine. I was its proprietor. With my overcoat wide open and the wind in my hair I walked around and for an hour or so presided over the bits of litter in the air—so much less than thirty years ago!—and the citizens bent against the weather, and the light inside the restaurants and the people at small tables looking at each other's faces and talking. The white flakes began to stick. By the time I entered Trump Tower, I'd had a long hard wet walk. I repaired myself in the restroom and found the right floor. At the ceremony my table was near the front—round, clothed in burgundy and surrounded by eight of us, the other seven much younger than I, a lively bunch, fun and full of wisecracks. And they seemed impressed to be sitting with me, and made sure I sat where I could see. All that was the good part.

Halfway through dessert the nerve in my back began to act up, and by the time I heard my name and started toward the podium, my right shoulder blade felt as if it were pressed against a hissing old New York steam-heat radiator. At the head of the vast room I held the medallion in my hand— that's what it was, rather than a trophy; an inscribed me- dallion three inches in diameter, good for a paperweight—and thanked a list of names I'd memorized, omitted any other remarks, and got back to our table just as another pain seized me, this one in the region of my bowels, and now I repented my curbside lunch, my delicious New York hot dogs, especially the second one, and without sitting down or even making an excuse I let this bout of indigestion carry me out of the room and down the halls to the men's lavatory, where I hardly had time to fumble the medallion into my lapel-pocket and get my jacket on the hook.

I sat down with my intestines in flames, first my body bearing this insult, and then my soul insulted, too, when someone came in and chose the stall next to mine. Our public toilets are just that—too public—the walls don't reach the floor. This other man and I could see each other's feet. Or at any rate, our black shoes, and the cuffs of our dark trousers.

After a minute his hand laid on the floor between us, there at the border between his space and mine, a square of toilet paper with an obscene proposition written on it, in words large and plain enough that I could read them whether I wanted to or not. In pain, I laughed. Not out loud.

I heard a small sigh from the next stall.

I didn't acknowledge his overture, and he didn't leave. He must have taken it that I had him under consideration. As long as I stayed, he had reason to hope. And I couldn't get away quite yet. My bowels churned and smoldered. Renegade signals from my spinal nerve hammered my shoulder and the full length of my right arm, down to the marrow.

The awards ceremony seemed to have ended. The men's room came to life—the door whooshing open, the run of voices coming in. Throats and faucets and footfalls. The spin of the paper towel dispenser.

Somewhere in here, a hand descended to the note on the floor, fingers touched it, raised it away. Soon after that the man, the toilet Casanova, was no longer beside me.

I stayed as I was, for how long I couldn't say. There were echoes. Silence. The urinals flushing themselves.

I raised myself upright, pulled my clothing together, made my way to the sinks.

One other man remained in the place. He stood at the sink beside mine as our faucets ran. I washed my hands. He washed his hands.

He was tall, with a distinctive head—wispy colorless hair like a baby's, and a skeletal face with thick red lips. I'd have known him anywhere.

"Carl Zane!"

He smiled in a small way. "Wrong. I'm Marshall Zane. I'm Carl's son."

"Sure, of course—he would have aged too!" This encounter had me going in circles. I'd finished washing my hands, and now I started washing them again. I forgot to introduce myself. "You look just like your dad," I said, "only twenty-five years ago. Are you here for the awards night?"

He nodded. "I'm with the Sextant Group."

"You followed in his footsteps."

"I did. I even worked for Castle and Forbes for a couple of years."

"How do you like that? And how's Carl doing? Is he here tonight?"

"He passed away three years ago. Went to sleep one night and never woke up."

"Oh. Oh, no." I had a moment—I have them sometimes— when the surroundings seemed bereft of any facts, and not even the smallest physical gesture felt possible. After the spell had passed, I said, "I'm sorry to hear that. He was a nice guy."

"At least it was painless," said the son of Carl Zane. "And as far as anyone knows, he went to bed happy that night."

We were talking to each other's reflections in the broad mirror. I made sure I didn't look elsewhere—at his trousers, his shoes. But for this occasion we men, every one of us, had dressed in dark trousers and black shoes.

"Well . . . enjoy your evening," the young man said.

I thanked him and said good night, and, as he tossed a wadded paper towel at the receptacle and disappeared out the door, I'm afraid I added, "Tell your father I said hello."

MERMAID

As I trudged up Fifth Avenue after this miserable interlude, I carried my shoulder like a bushel-bag of burning kindling and could hardly stay upright the three blocks to my hotel. It was really snowing now, and it was Saturday night. The sidewalk was crowded. People came at me forcing themselves against the weather, their shoulders hunched, their coats pinched shut, flakes battering their faces, and though the faces were dark, I felt I saw into their eyes.

I came awake in the unfamiliar room I didn't know how much later, and, if this makes sense, it wasn't the pain in my shoulder that woke me, but its departure. I lay bathed in relief.

Beyond my window, a thick layer of snow covered the ledge. I became aware of a hush of anticipation, a tremendous surrounding absence. I got out of bed, dressed in my clothes, and went out to look at the city.

It was I think around 1 a.m. Snow six inches deep had fallen. Park Avenue looked smooth and soft—not one vehicle had disturbed its surface. The city was almost completely stopped, its very few sounds muffled yet perfectly distinct from one another: a rumbling snowplow somewhere, a car's horn, a man on another street shouting several faint syllables. I tried counting up the years since I'd seen snow. Eleven or twelve—Denver, and it had been exactly the same, exactly like this. One lone taxi glided up Park Avenue through the virgin white, and I hailed it and asked the driver to find any restaurant open for business. I looked out the back window at the brilliant silences falling from the streetlamps, and at our fresh black tracks disappearing into the infinite—the only proof of Park Avenue; I'm not sure how the cabbie kept to the road. He took me to a small diner off Union Square, where I had a wonderful breakfast among a handful of miscellaneous wanderers like myself, New Yorkers with their large, historic faces, every one of whom, delivered here without an explanation, seemed invaluable. I paid and left and set out walking back toward midtown. I'd bought a pair of weatherproof dress shoes just before leaving San Diego, and I was glad. I looked for places where I was the first to walk and kicked at the powdery snow. A piano playing a Latin tune drew me through a doorway into an atmosphere of sadness: a dim tavern, a stale smell, the piano's weary melody, and a single customer, an ample, attractive woman with abundant blond hair. She wore an evening gown. A light shawl covered her shoulders. She seemed poised and self-possessed, though it was possible, also, that she was weeping.

I let the door close behind me. The bartender, a small old black man, raised his eyebrows, and I said, "Scotch rocks, Red Label." Talking, I felt discourteous. The piano played in the gloom of the farthest corner. I recognized the melody as a Mexican traditional called "Maria Elena." I couldn't see the musician at all. In front of the piano a big tenor saxophone rested upright on a stand. With no one around to play it, it seemed like just another of the personalities here: the invisible pianist, the disenchanted old bartender, the big glamorous blonde, the shipwrecked, solitary saxophone . . . And the man who'd walked here through the snow . . . And as soon as the name of the song popped into my head I thought I heard a voice say, "Her name is Maria Elena." The scene had a moonlit, black-and-white quality. Ten feet away at her table the blond woman waited, her shoulders back, her face raised. She lifted one hand and beckoned me with her fingers. She was weeping. The lines of her tears sparkled on her cheeks. "I am a prisoner here," she said. I took the chair across from her and watched her cry. I sat upright, one hand on the table's surface and the other around my drink. I felt the ecstasy of a dancer, but I kept still.

WHIT

My name would mean nothing to you, but there's a very good chance you're familiar with my work. Among the many TV ads I wrote and directed, you'll remember one in particular.

In this animated 30-second spot, you see a brown bear chasing a gray rabbit. They come one after the other over a hill toward the view—the rabbit is cornered, he's crying, the bear comes to him—the rabbit reaches into his waistcoat pocket and pulls out a dollar bill and gives it to the bear. The bear looks at this gift, sits down, stares into space. The music stops, there's no sound, nothing is said, and right there the little narrative ends, on a note of complete uncertainty. It's an advertisement for a banking chain. It sounds ridiculous, I know, but that's only if you haven't seen it. If you've seen it, the way it was rendered, then you know that it was a very unusual advertisement. Because it referred, really, to nothing at all, and yet it was actually very moving.

Advertisements don't try to get you to fork over your dough by tugging irrelevantly at your heart-strings, not as a rule. But this one broke the rules, and it worked.

It brought the bank chain many new customers. And it excited a lot of commentary and won several awards— every award I ever won, in fact, I won for that ad. It ran in both halves of the twenty-second Super Bowl, and people still remember it.

You don't get awards personally. They go to the team. To the agency. But your name attaches to the project as a matter of workplace lore—"Whit did that one." (And that would be me, Bill Whitman.) "Yes, the one with the rabbit and the bear was Whit's."

Credit goes first of all to the banking firm who let this strange message go out to potential customers, who sought to start a relationship with a gesture so cryptic. It was better than cryptic—mysterious, untranslatable. I think it pointed to orderly financial exchange as the basis of harmony. Money tames the beast. Money is peace. Money is civilization. The end of the story is money.

I won't mention the name of the bank. If you don't remember the name, then it wasn't such a good ad after all.

If you watched any primetime television in the 1980s, you've almost certainly seen several other ads I wrote or directed or both.

I crawled out of my twenties leaving behind a couple of short, unhappy marriages, and then I found Elaine. Twenty-five years last June, and two daughters. Have I loved my wife? We've gotten along. We've never felt like congratulating ourselves.

I'm just shy of sixty-three. Elaine's fifty-two but seems older. Not in her looks, but in her attitude of complacence. She lacks fire. Seems interested mainly in our two girls. She keeps in close contact with them. They're both grown. They're harmless citizens. They aren't beautiful or clever.

Before the girls started grade school, we left New York and headed west in stages, a year in Denver (too much winter), another in Phoenix (too hot), and finally San Diego. What a wonderful city. It's a bit more crowded each year, but still. Completely wonderful. Never regretted coming here, not for an instant. And financially it all worked out. If we'd stayed in New York I'd have made a lot more money, but we'd have needed a lot more, too.

Last night Elaine and I lay in bed watching TV, and I asked her what she remembered. Not much. Less than I. We have a very small TV that sits on a dresser across the room. Keeping it going provides an excuse for lying awake in bed.

I note that I've lived longer in the past, now, than I can expect to live in the future. I have more to remember than I have to look forward to. Memory fades, not much of the past stays, and I wouldn't mind forgetting a lot more of it.

Once in a while I lie there, as the television runs, and I read something wild and ancient from one of several collections of folk tales I own. Apples that summon sea maidens, eggs that fulfill any wish, and pears that make people grow long noses that fall off again. Then sometimes I get up and don my robe and go out into our quiet neighborhood looking for a magic thread, a magic sword, a magic horse.

THE STARLIGHT

ON IDAHO

~~~~

Dear Jennifer Johnston,

Well, to catch you up on things, the last four years have really kicked my ass. I try to get back to that point I was at in the fifth grade where you sent me a note with a heart on it said "Dear Mark I really like you" and I turned that note over and wrote on the back of it "Do you like me or love me?" and you made me a new note with twenty hearts on it and sent it back down the aisles and it said "I love you! I love you! I love you! I love you!" I would count there to be about fifteen or sixteen hooks in my belly with lines heading off into the hands of people I haven't seen since a long time back, and that's one of them. But just to catch you up. In the last five years I've been arrested about eight times, shot twice, not twice on one occasion, but once on two different occasions, etc etc and I think I got run over once but I don't even remember it. I've loved a couple thousand women but I think you're number one on the list. That's all folks, over and out.

Cass (in 5th grade you used to call me Mark—full name Mark Cassandra)

PS—Where, you might ask, am I? Funny that you asked. After all those adventures I'm at an undisclosed location right back here once again in Ukiah, the Armpit of Northern California.

Cass

~~~~~

Dear old buddy and beloved sponsor Bob,

Now hear the latest from the Starlight Addiction Recovery Center on Idaho Avenue, in its glory days better known as the Starlight Motel. I believe you might have holed up here once or twice. Yes I believe you might have laid up drunk in room 8, this very one I'm sitting in at this desk writing this letter, which is one of the few I'll actually be mailing because I need a few things which are in that box in your closet, anyway I hope they're still there. I think there's a pair of jeans and I think there's a few pairs of socks, and in fact if you would just bring the whole box. I'm down to one of everything, except for two of these socks, which are both white, but they're not the same brand. My good old boots collapsed, but I have been given an excellent pair of secondhand running shoes here. But I am writing to tell you this—that I am not running anywhere, I am standing my ground, I intend to do the deal and here's why. Because the last four years have positively kicked my ass. In the last four years I have been shot, jailed, declared insane, etc . . .

and even though I'm just thirty-two years old I'm the only person I've ever met who's actually ever been in a coma. I have been asked over and over by medical people who probably know what they're talking about "Why aren't you dead?"

Wow, I think I just took a nap. They've got us on Antabuse here and sometimes, blip, you just fade out and dream. In a few days that's supposed to pass.

They won't let me call you but I'm pretty sure they'll let you come to Family Group, which is on Sunday, two to four. Before I mail this I will check if it's OK for you to come. I wouldn't mind seeing a friendly face in the circle there.

I'm not the type to trudge along, I'm the type to come shooting off the block, get twenty yards ahead of everybody else, and go stumbling and sprawling off onto the sidelines with a collapsed lung. And pretty soon I hear the others, here they come, I hear them trudging steadily along on their Road to Happy Destiny.

I've got to have somebody reminding me to stay in my lane and take it easy, that's where my buddy Bob C comes in, he's my sponsor in the AA, but the thing about your sponsor is you've got to call him. I don't like to call him. He's always got something wise and reasonable to say.

So if he turned up with my box of stuff and two cents of input for the Family Group discussion, what a relief.

Cass

~~~~~

Dear Old Dad and Dear Grandma,

I'm sitting here in this room at this desk at the Starlight Addiction Recovery Center writing letters to everybody I know. I've got about a dozen hooks in my heart, I'm following the lines back to where they go. I hope somebody up there knows I'm sincere about this, I could certainly use a little help, but I might as well announce right here that I'm not about to get on my knees, because I've never been that way, and if your pal Jesus is waiting around for somebody like me to do something like that before he comes down off the cross, I'd say he can quit waiting. Damn this place and everybody in it, I mean I have just about had it with rehabilitation. The thing is group therapy has just made the kinks in my mind all that tighter. It's basically a circle of terrified bullshitters kissing this guy's ass named Jerry. If you're late to a session they lock you out, late to a second session you're expelled back on the street, I mean let's all just step one step back and take a look at the fact that I was never in the Army because I cannot stand exactly that kind of discipline. Oh yeah. I am just pissed off, and that's about it. I have to spend two hours every single night in this room at this desk considering these hooks in my heart and writing down my life history, which we each go up at the two-week point and read to them, read to all the others, sit there in a chair, read your history of the downfall of your pitiful self to a circle of ghosts. I may or may not get around to doing it. Right now I'm just filling a notebook with jazz, waiting for my handwriting to improve itself. Like I say though—I am I am I am sincere. I am sincere. Here's some pretty good evidence—this is my third time in rehab, but my first time to make it past four days.

Well Grandma that was entertaining what you pulled in Family Group last Sunday but ridiculous. Come on back sometime but keep a lid on it, Okay?

I'm through being the one to explain this family to each other. I know how in your eyes Grandma it's like every one of us is the runt from a litter of geniuses, we just need extra feeding and we'll sprout. But the total number of times it adds up to that the jail doors have clanged on us is pretty impressive Grandma, and those are the statistics, they speak for themselves. Whatever these people in this rehab are doing to help me I think we should pause and consider it. I'm shocked to hear myself say that, but the last four years my habits have drug me behind them over some pretty rough ground and now I'm teachable. Let's set our ideas aside and just listen. I thought you were listening at the Family Day group session on Sunday but I'm sorry, it turned out you were more like laying in wait to pounce like a slobbering cougar on poor Jerry, who I happen to despise, but he's the one clean and sober three years while meanwhile I'm the one drunk not a week ago. I've just got nothing left to say. I get around a mirror and it isn't pretty.

I don't need grandmotherly help, I need trained and certified counselors to point a few things out. And I can't have my Grandma at Family Group red-dogging the whole discussion and preaching about Jesus Christ and Satan, or anyway the last thirty minutes of a two-hour group, that's how much time you took up jiving on Heaven and Hell, thanks a million. Luckily Jerry has a sense of humor. Thank you for representing the Cassandra family in a most standout way. I am not surrounded by demons here. These are trained and certified counselors.

I am through explaining this family to each other. It's G-damn ridiculous is what it is. I guess I can swear here as you won't be receiving this as I won't be sending it. Do you remember when the Starlight was a motel? I remember when it was a motel and whores used to sit out on the bench at the bus stop across the street, really miserable gals with blotchy skin and dents in their head after getting run out of San Francisco. You have to be pretty down on your luck to get knocked off the market in the Tenderloin. I mean you wouldn't cross the street for them, but I guess once in a while some desperate character from one of these rooms in the Starlight would make the journey. Do you know what? I've had one or two minutes here when I might've done it myself. But the whores are gone, the bus-stop benches are empty. I don't think the bus runs past here no more.

I mean this is not a family to get their coat of arms tattooed on your chest. Do you remember when Bro broke his girl-friend's nose in the living room and said "There, I rest my case." Do you remember when Dad scooped his hand down in his soggy cereal and just sat there staring at nothing for about twenty-two minutes with a glop of it in his hand? Do you remember when John got his picture in the papers in Dallas being arrested, and he sent it to us in the mail like it was really something to write home about? You know what I remember most about that picture? The borders were all ragged because he had to tear it out of the page with his fingers. My oldest brother is somebody who the state of Texas won't let him possess scissors.

Incidentally, if this rehab program works and if I get it to-gether, if I reach a point of balance, I will enroll in college.

That's not what I started out to say, but if I get so I can look people in the eye, get so I can make change and carry on conversations, I will get a part-time job and enroll in college. But as for my Grandma, as for last Family Group day

~~~~~

Dear Pope John Paul

Do you have two first names, or is Paul your last name, like you're Mr. Paul.

And I know it's not just dumb luck, I know I ordered the circumstances.

At first I was interested in getting high, I liked to laugh at nothing and get my feet crossed and go down on my ass. Then later it was torture, but it was a button I could push to destroy the known world.

I mean it's like I get that glass as far as just touching against my lower lip, and next thing I know I'm on the Ghost-Bus to Vegas. There's a certain power in that you know, it's like if you don't like the movie you're in you just grab this jug going by and it takes you and flings you into a completely different story.

What do they feed you when you're the Pope? Try the stuff around here sometime. For lunch they give you a marshmaller and a coffee bean. It's a salvage yard for people who totaled their souls called the Starlight Recovery Center in Ukiah, California, on Idaho Avenue. Ah hell what's wrong with me? I won't be sending no letter to the Pope.

But I'm telling you I think I've been dealing with the Devil and I could use some expert coaching. There really is a Devil, he really does talk to me, and I think it might be coming from some Antabuse giving me side effects, but be that as it may I need to know the rules. So far I think I've found out that I don't have to obey his orders, I can just ignore him, sort of, but if I keep pissing him off is he going to get after my people?

Mark Cassandra

~~~~~

Dear Satan,
Senor Mr. Business, you are one big fuckin bubble and I'd hate to be there when you go POP because then I'd get a lot of really rank stuff on me.

I mean I'm here to change or die trying but all I can think about is if this was still the old Starlight, the Motel Of Bad Dreams, I'd scrape together a couple hundred dollars and lay up here drunk until they smelled my corpse and broke the lock. But everything changes, and the Starlight's all new and different, and I'd better get new and different too, and find a better way of filling up than alcohol. I like the thing this guy Wendell was saying in group, he put out the idea of pouring in the right thoughts into our poison thinking—like pouring good water into a glass of dirty water—until I'm filling up and spilling over and just keep going like that till I'm running clean.

My Grandma puts it that Cass if you keep drinking your babies will come out crosseyed, and you'll end up buried in a strange town with your name spelled wrong on your grave.

~~~~~

Dear Sis

Here I am—yep—again—same old story.

But this time I swear it's feeling different. You're the one person I've never jived, so that's as far as I'll go with that one. It's feeling different, that's as much as I'll swear to.

If you want to come to Family Group you can. I have had one Family Group but nobody came but dear old Grandma and that led to an incident. I realize you're stuck in Dallas but if you come home for a vacation, I wouldn't mind seeing a friendly face. And if it was my sister Marigold, I'd be smiling. Marigold, sister Marigold. My noble young petunia. It's every Sunday, Two PM. You'll do better than Grandma I'd lay odds. She didn't have a word to say, not until about three-fifteen. Family Group goes for two hours—the wives, husbands, children, any close people, they all come for group therapy. Mostly sitting with rods up their butts and every face pulled tight, nobody knows if they're about to get ratted out, get their covers yanked. Playing it close, in other words, as far as the twisted little games they play with their loved ones. Jerry asking "What would you say to your loved one," and they say, "I don't know. I pass," like that. But this one guy Calvin who's been in these places plenty, he looks at his wife when it's their turn and just comes out with it—he looked at her—"I love you." He was looking straight at her and he was sniffling, crying. She looked at him and went "I—I—I—" She looked at him like he was trying to get her to jump from a high-rise fire to save herself, but she just couldn't quite say something real. "I don't care about these people" Calvin said "I don't give a damn about anything except that I love you." . . . "I love you too," she said, "Baby I love you too!" and while we all watched, and I mean

Grandma too, this couple were embracing and crying for about five minutes. I don't know how much long-run good it does to be doing that, but I tell you this, it certainly livens up the Family Day when you see that kind of thing happening, it just keeps the whole thing fascinating. So I was going to tell you about Grandma. So Jerry there, they call him the counselor or facilitator, Jerry, at the start of the session, he comes out with a pretty harmless lecture about how the booze isn't anybody's fault, it might be in the genes, in the blood, inherited. Grandma's sitting there like Sunday school with her hands in her lap for I'd say one and one half hours, never a peep until I notice she's cutting her eyes at Jerry, I mean they're down to burning slits, man, and right in the middle of somebody else's stuff she just lays into him with something to the effect of "Jerry if that's really your name I think you'd climb a tree and tell a lie before you'd stand on the ground and tell the natural truth." Jerry's going wuh wuh wuh and she just draws up another lungful of this good old California air which she always claims is poison and says "Do you mean to say you're going to pin all this on me his grandmother and on my ancestors too when we are good Nantahala Mountain people who never should've left North Carolina and my husband wrote speeches for the Mayor of Odessa Texas and our blood's as good as yours and you say it's passing down alcoholic generations like the sins of the fathers?" and rolls right along with a whole bitter lecture of her own about "you've got to stand on your own two feet and not blame your relatives for your own miserable mistakes" with her face three inches from Jerry's. He looked like he was ready to go out and hang himself. I enjoyed that.

Needless to say, the subject of Jesus came up in this discussion, right about thirteen seconds into it. "The Alcoholic Anonymous is an arm of Satan, you might as well get that through your head, and shut your trap," and so on.

Like I say, they hold Family Group on Sundays at two pm. Two to Four pm. And I'm required to be in attendance like I say, and if I don't have any family at Family Group, what's the point? So you're invited. I mean if they ever let you out of Dallas.

Over and out. Over and out. They give us Antabuse in here, and it makes you sleepy. Over and out.

~~~~~

Dear Bro
I got too near the edge of the ride and flew off.

I am done done done man. Yeah, get out your fork.

You know it will be my 33rd birthday next October but in just the last couple years I've had at least three of those experiences where afterward you wake up and remember nothing and some medical expert is attaching back on various parts of you and saying "Son you are lucky to be breathing."

But did you ever think that maybe there actually is a devil and he actually does get his claws in certain people and they actually do get dragged through the garbage of an evil life on their way to actually going to hell?

Here's the thing, Luke. Last year I told you how I went to Texas. Houston, Dallas, Odessa, all of that. But I didn't tell you that since then, since the last time I saw you, when you behaved like an atomic shit-bomb in the harmless home of our dear old Dad and Grandma, since that night when you broke your girlfriend's nose in the living room in front of the whole family and calmly said, "There, I rest my case," I went to the good old prison in good old Gatesville to see good old Mom.

Yeah. I went to see our mother.

She shrank to a dot right while I was looking at her.

She said,
I'd take a nap and at some point I'd wake up,

Because I'd hear a dog whimpering, and I'd wake up,
And the dog was inside me, a puppy
Was crying to break its little heart inside me.

She said,
Your father rose a little bit above my origins
But I sank you all back down to my level

Fujiyama Mama, that was her song. Remember?
I'm a fujiyama mama and I'm just about to blow my top.
and when I start erupting
I don't know when I'm ever gonna stop

Is that a real song, or did she make that up?

Excuse me, I have to burn this page and write a letter to
God while it's on fire. Question is, God, where are you?
What the fuck on earth do you think you're doing, man?
We are in HELL down here, HELL down here, HELL. You
know? Where's Superman?

When Grandma showed up here for a demented visit she
took me aside and says, "You are surrounded by demons.
God has his hand around your guts and he is dragging you
out of Hell." Well, this is the longest ride out of Hell I ever
heard about, and if I'm out of Hell, whose meat is that I

smell frying? God has put his feet up and screwed the head off a Bud and has drifted off into a nap while I sit here burning and stinking on the barbecue.

~~~~~

Dear Melanie,

—you know, I'm glad I met you and heard the story from you in group about your daughter dying, and your purse. It would have made me even sicker if it was just a story about some person I could only think about. Like somebody I could only imagine. But it isn't as hard since I got to really meet you. And hear about it in person. Because you have a sweet sincere quality, you're bouncy, smiley, young for 61 years, and no matter how hard you've been knocked around I saw you in a light, you're beautiful.

These last four years have chewed several giant holes right through me. I thought I was finished before. But that was minimum damage compared to this.

Your fellow inmate
Mark Cassandra (Cass)

~~~~~

Dear Satan

I did not enjoy it at your Jamboree last night

~~~~~

Dear Doctor

I'm gonna roll a cigaret and I'd like to light it and get through the entire thing in a state of sanity.

I did see the Devil one time.

~~~~~

Dear Doc,

To continue, this woman in group, Melanie, she's old enough to be an old lady but she's not, she's sweet, soft, very easy in her soul, it seems like. She starts off talking soft and matter of fact—then it's getting to be a regular thing, somebody who starts out like that suddenly breaks down, full of tragedy—she, Melanie, lost her daughter and two grandkids in a fire last year. "My daughter was a Good Christian girl. Two fine good beautiful kids, she raised them right, raised them Christian." Lost them in an apartment fire. Now. Here's one for you Doctor—

While she, Melanie, slept in the waiting room at the Burn Unit and her daughter died, somebody snuck out their hand and stole her purse. Took the money out and threw the purse in the trashcan. She found it in the trashcan later, after they told her that her daughter and two grandkids were dead.

In group the other night a guy just like me said, "I Woke up in Vegas sticky, broke, and confused"—a perfect description of that place—I've never GONE there, just WOKE UP there. That guy was funny. Reminded me of Gary Cooper, a real cowpoke down on his luck in the smelly cities that ate the prairie. How long was he around, two days? I heard he went to the Redwood Motel two blocks east of here at the corner of Fourth, and he's shacking up with some Mexican kid, not a girl, a boy, I mean that's the trouble inside him, he's got two acts going at once, he's a rope-em ride-em cowboy and he's a happy little sodomizer, and it's shorting him out. That's what we gotta do is get down to just one story, the true person we are, and live it all the way out.

I'm getting depressed. Depressed. I think this Antabuse is going wrong on me. You said we'd feel run down or sleepy two or three days to start with, but you forgot to say prepare to fall down through a trap door in the bottom of your soul. Also I've heard people talking right outside my window who aren't there when I go look. Around other folks, I mean real folks, folks who are really there, I feel absolutely fine. They talk, I talk, everything appears as normal. Get in this room and shut the door behind me and I'm alone with somebody who's not there.

~~~~~

Dear Friends and Neighbors in the Universe
Dear Rolling Stone and TV Guide
I think I need to tell you I am totally out of Kools. Some kind person has donated a whole can of Bugler that we can roll out of, but I tell you what, Bugler smoke burns like fire from your lips on down to the pit of your lungs. So—if you brought me a couple packs of my brand. Know what I mean? Kools.

I have written thousands upon thousands of these letters and the reason I don't run out of ink—I don't think I'm actually writing too many of them down. Or any of them. I think I'm just wandering hiking marching all around this room like it's a small tiny mental institution hallucinating.

Hey. About this Antabuse. I think I'm Christ. I hear the Devil. And so it's, "Get back in your room." Stupidest thing I ever heard.

That is so Eddie.

That is so Eddie, man.

They are the Eddiest most ridiculous people that if you pull this letter up to your ear you can hear me laughing at them like a ciyoot.

They are a bunch of Eddies and so ridiculous flat faces and flat minds.

These last four years. Sometimes I wonder if I didn't die. And I'm really dead, and this is Purgatory, Heaven, or Hell. And it's up to me which one.

One thing is you don't get me to do things. I don't listen. Might as well shut up. I am not a slave.

Where I just was . . . was the Road of Hell. Black boiling dirt and burning diesel smoke. Nothing burns hot as diesel. People by the side runover squashed killed and dead. Devil laughing so close I saw the veins in his teeth. You won't get ahold of me. My ticket says to Texas. He rolled the stone aside and in the cave the mysteries flitted like bats and insects, here the answers to everything, said the Devil, like UFO's and life beyond the grave. Like what was elvis thinking, what was elvis thinking and feeling in those last dark days? Like just who masterminded JFK? And the cave was his mouth like a bathroom full of stink and his tongue popped with cheap sweat. Yeah boy he dragged me down to his jamboree. Dragged me down through the toilet formerly known as my life. Down through this nest of talking spiders known as my head. Down through the bottom of my grave with my name spelled wrong on the stone. Standing on his stump shouting jive. Jest get a whiff of sulphur and wet fear! Come breathe these rank aromas for the purposes of course of scientific inquiry alone! The mayor is inside already! Come! It's all respectable! Satan says The gamblers shake the dice, and shake I the gamblers, Snake eyes in Paradise! Satan shouts I run the jamboree, and Hollywood and Vegas, and start all the wars, vampire breather of the baby's breath, I the worker of the strings to jerk the fools dancing, Glue-huffers, jelly-rollers, paint-suckers, Bikers, truckers, cowboys, teachers, preachers, About a million hipsters hooked on dope, Shaky alkies with their nerves burned up, Hey God where is you you ain't nowhere, We search for some faint signal from your power . . . All that just now, right now, while I'm writing it down.

Not yer boy,
Cass

Dr so and-so

I forget your name. Listen to me. I can't get this across to anybody in this ridiculous pathetic excuse for a rehab but I have to tell you I think this Antabuse you gave us is backfiring with some serious side-effects. I lie on that bed over there and my mood goes black and then I can feel my mind, my actual mind, pulling itself in two. I hear the Devil laughing, and I hear him ordering me to kill people. Don't worry, he's been running me all my life but he can't tell me straight out what to do, there's no way I would ever take a direct order from anybody, that's why I never went into the military. But if you read the papers you see every day where somebody just jumps up and chops the baby's head off, and I have to tell you there's been some of that in my very own family. My mother when I was four years old went psycho herself and has been in prison for twenty-eight years in Gatesville, Texas, and prison has not in any way reformed her. She should've gotten out by now, but she won't behave and they just keep adding on.

Last week here in Number 8 I had a train-jumper wino roommate with slashed-up shoes and a tattoo on his arm said Eat Fuck Kill. That was his complete statement. Never said hello, never said good-bye. Never took off his shoes. Here two days and then up and gone. He was all hate. I've got to get sober or I'll get that way where every

breath you breathe just stinks and it only takes one minute in a new town before you're mad enough to leave.
When the Devil gets that last hook in your heart, then he
starts yanking you town to town. My grandma tells the
truth about the Devil. Well, all right, when she says "the
Devil's yanking on you" it sounds like somebody's grandma
babbling, but when it's happening to you it's snakes crawl-
ing into every orifice, and you can't move to stop them
getting in.

My sponsor Bob Cornfield dropped around finally with a
box of my stuff, not much, a small box and the contents
inside still rattled. He gets his cigaret going standing here in
this room, room 8, looking around like he invented the
place. These AA guys are faking about eighty percent of it,
but let's just hang on to the truth, they're clean and sober
and I'm the one woke up with his head in the toilet not two
weeks back. I think to see me here made him sad, but he
won't show pity. Not allowed.

I told him I feel like I might be Jesus Christ and the
Devil is sending me messages, and he said "You can't be the
Second Coming, cause I am." I think it was a joke, but I've
lost my talent for humor. It scared me.

Let's just face the music and the facts. Somebody's going
out of my mind.

Your patient at the Starlight,
Mark Cassandra (just call me Cass)

~~~~~

To dr in charge of antabuse complaints:
Meanwhile, all these people in group, I hate them. Maybe oh
well some of them aren't so bad, I don't know which ones
though. OK I like so-and-so. First several days I was here she
was like a robot in group. Carolina that's her name. Changed
her shirt and pants but never varied her performance. This
was Linda's group, afternoon group, each time Linda says
how do you feel Carolina, what's your story Carolina, and
every time she gives back the same speech, you could make
it into a song, same thing over and over the first five days,
not bad looking, about 40 or 45, kind of chubby but in a
sexy way, made herself up just right, like a doll, every morning, like this is the Riviera Rehab, man. And she wore these
middle-age type big-enough shorts, but these little-girl white
patent leather shoes. Singing, "My husband left me fifteen
years ago with a woman from the firm he worked for, just
left me flat, and every morning for the last fifteen years I
wake up and think about those two and I get sick way down
inside my stomach. Most mornings, to tell you the truth, I
have to vomit about it." Woman in charge, Linda, says "You

mean you feel angry." "No, I'm not angry, I'm just a little disgusted at the behavior." Every day Linda says, "You mean you feel angry." "But I'm not angry, Linda, and I don't believe you've heard me, for you keep on asking that question." Finally she says "Linda, I AM NOT ANGRY LINDA YOU FUCKIN CUNT-FACE BITCH WHORE" and so on, and ripping out of the room, down the hall and clear across the courtyard screaming like an F-16. She's gone. We're all sitting there in that room shocked deaf and dumb, as shocked as if she'd just blown herself to bits before our eyes. Well, I assumed we all assumed what I assumed, that she'd never be back, she'd keep marching through the gates and stop a taxi or stick her thumb out, one of those, and be gone gone gone. Like my roommate Eat Fuck Kill. But the very next morning here's Carolina sitting in her usual chair, and I have to say, her eyes were so much light, like somebody's put two suction cups on the sockets and sucked out all the dark and sadness. "Now to get to the truth" she said, "Hey everybody, I was a whore in Denver before I got married, at Madam Lafayette's for almost six years, till technology and the Mob ruined the business with credit cards and massage parlors, and then I got married, and now I'm divorced, and I don't know what else to say. I didn't want to face how I felt about my husband and that bitch of his. I feel a lot better now that I know I hate those two for running off and sticking me with the tab for the rent and phone and the whole middle class life. I think they live in Mexico. I hope they get a few diseases that make them miserable." Big smile. Having fun. She spent her whole twenties in this old-fashion place in Denver with a piano and a Madam, strolling around joshing with the clients.

I mean that's how it is. Group therapy isn't some gigantic mystery. We alkies are just a tangle of lies like the insides of a golf ball. You start cutting into one little rubber band in that mess like how do you really feel about your husband shafting you, and the whole ball starts unraveling and whizzing around the room.

Now look look look. I know we're here to get honest. And I feel I've been doing it the last few months, even before I landed here again, but I still don't see Mr. AA Breakthrough in the mirror. I see something lurking over my shoulder. You know who it is. Devil been talking to me. Telling me to kill everybody in here. Laughing. I hear these things clearly but I still feel sane, sane. Like I know I shouldn't be hearing these things, so what is the cause? Am I torching out on Antabuse? Why do I think I might be Jesus Christ and I'm supposed to come here and suffer, really suffer, and why do I think every-body's looking at me because they know this about me? Why does the radio seem to know what I'm thinking and pick up the conversation right in the middle of my thoughts when I pass the window in Jerry's office and he's listening to the news? I say "I'm not killing anybody, Satan," and the radio says "The President's order has been disobeyed." If I am Jesus Christ and I'm going to Hell, then I want you to say so. You're the one I'm asking, Dr. whatsyername. And if I'm not Jesus Christ, then I want you to get me off these pills because they're obviously running me the wrong way.

I'd like to get through a whole cigaret without thinking crazy. I don't remember my previous goals but the goal right now is to get through this cigaret man without starting up Satan's Jamboree.

Still me, still in here, still your patient, so what's the problem,
Mark Cassandra room 8

~~~~

Dear Dr Cusa,
Thanks for taking me off the Antabuse. Every hour I feel more down to the ground. I don't know why I didn't have the balls to just stop taking it without your say so. It's like I know I don't know what's good for me. The last four years. Wow. Thanks for taking me off that stuff. The world has been saved.

~~~~~~

Dear Satan

You think I didn't recognize you that time?

It was outside of Harold's Tavern downtown about three-four minutes ago. Come out onto the street right after Happy Hour exactly at the moment the sun descended.

There he is. Guy leaning up against the wall in an alley with his knee bent back, sole of his foot against the wall like we used to do, we kids who thought we were so tough.

What do you want? I said.

All of you is mine already, he said. So what difference does it make what I want?

I said, Are you a messenger of God?

Worse, he said.

I said, What could be worse than a messenger of God?

~~~~~~

Dear Satan

Yeah, they took me off the Antabuse. That Antabuse was your last thing. Well it didn't work. Everybody thinks you're just this amazingly cool cat in a striped suit in a ragtop Caddy suckin on a cellphone, licking fire from your fingers, plotting the downfall. Pulling on the strings. But you got no strings. Not one of these strings from my heart-hooks lead off into your evil hands.

These hooks lead out from my heart to the hearts of people I love. So get outa my Caddy, Daddy. Ain't neither one of us driving this thing. Who's driving it is and I feel like a genuine pussy saying it but a Power Greater Than Myself.

Mark Cassandra, a more or less Christian

~~~~~

Dear Brother John
John I'm gonna come and see you—are you in a regular prison yet? Or do they have you drooling on a ward somewhere?

~~~~~

Dear John the Strangest Of All us Cassandras,

And oh say there incidentally I do mean it—you're the strangest of all us Cassandras, more strange than Dad, more strange even than Mom in prison. More strange than me too, don't matter how many times they shoot me. More strange than Bro, but just by a hair.

I'm writing letters to everybody I can think of. You and Bro are getting a little ink here. May the cops never catch him, and now that you're caught, may they treat you gently and release you in the near future. I'm writing letters to each one of you lucky winners who has a hook in my heart. Every time your heart beats I can feel a little jerk, just a little something. Whether you like it or not, that's love. Love for the idiot Grandma. Love for the medicated Father. Love for the brother on the run and for the brother and the mother in prison in Gatesville. May the visions of your heart be blessed. That's what I heard a preacher say on TV one time. May the blessings of the sun and the rain find us out.

Love for the sister who should divorce us all. Love for sister Marigold who should divorce us once and for all.

John, I believe you and Marigold were the two of us not to get mixed up seriously with substances. She's turned out so golden. Then you on the other hand, well, no substances are required. A few bad days on Planet E can warp you just fine. And Mom. Whew. She sucked in enough stuff to count for the whole family's warpage and plenty more. I was tiny, but I remember. She used to sit there in her blue recliner, snorting glue or sucking Sterno through a sponge or whuffing spray-paint through a sock. And failing to understand the television. And praying to hallucinations. And getting results. To me she wasn't so much of a mother, really, John. More of a fairy tale. Kind of a legend. Mom in Prison in Texas. A myth. Mom. Prison. Texas. Finally I went to see her. Brought my birth certificate and everything, they couldn't keep me out. Guard takes me through to a room says wait a while son, comes back in twenty minutes and he says, "Your Mom's inside," and yeah, That's what brings me here today, to see the famous unremembered person face-to-face . . . Nothing happened. I didn't feel a thing. I got no relief. She's a flumpy Mexican gal in a white uniform looks like she cleans rooms. Gray hair with a couple black streaks. Medicated to keep her mind off suicide. It worked too well. She was deeply content. A freight train bearing down on her wouldn't get a response. Being around her re-laxed me. Like resting in the shade by a wide, flat pond. She thought Dad was dead. What? No, Dad's not *dead*! He's not? No, Mom, he isn't dead, he's just upstairs. Mostly crying and watching television. She says Yeah he never was much good around the house. Which wouldna been so bad, I guess, except he never went anywhere else. Just hung around making up poems and never writing them down. What's California like? . . . Mysterious, Mom. All filled with shiny mist. And foggy sunshine . . . God, that sounds nice, but oh well, I'll never get there. Listen, she said, what is the problem with you boys? . . . What is the PROBLEM?

Maybe you notice I'm a walking talking Piece of Shit,
mother. She leaned close and looked at my face. You could
see her mind wiggling right through her eyeballs. Then she
had this flash of clear light. Said "Sorry doesn't get it, I realize that." I said Lady, that's what I come for.

Old Bro wandered back to Ukiah last summer sometime.
Brother Luke hisself with his ass showing through the pockets of his jeans and still putting everybody else down. I
wouldn't have recognized him on the street. I'd need a
flashlight and a map to find Luke's eyes in that poor sick
mean sad face. Came back to make trouble for his old girlfriend, did you ever know her? Susie? Bro says "poking
around in her stool for my broken heart." Lives in mud and
gonna bring the whole world down to taste it. He wants the
world to realize how for some this life comes hard, it's all
uphill, they just get tired, they just get so weary, they just
want the cops to carry them away to that sweet land called
jail and tuck them into their trundle-beds. What I wish is
that he could come to a place like this and hear a couple
people tell the truth. It's inspiring, Brother John. It's fantas-
tic how men and women come out from under these lifelong
lies. Roll them off their backs and say phew, whoosh, long
time carrying that mother. And the things they tell. The shit
they've done. The blood they've swum through. The fool
moves, the lucky chances, the wins and losses, all the burnt

down houses, all the children wailing in the storms, the lucky hit at the last minute, or turning their back on the hearts they broke over and over, or getting busted on their birthday, or thinking they're dead then waking up with the sun all warm on their face, and hitching home cross-country in the rain just in time to say that one important thing before their father takes his dying breath, or getting there too late and saying it to his grave instead. This one speaker Howard had us all frozen up, we listened to him stock-still for forty-five minutes. He started out simple, comes out of high-school, tries the infantry, finds the service kind of boring without a war. Drinking on leave and weekends. Gets his discharge, goes to Santa Rosa Community College. Going for a business degree. Drinking on weekends. Itchy and discontented. One night, he has this friend who's a cop in SR, guy says, ride along with us and get a taste. He says two hours into the ride I'm feeling like I never felt. These guys tell a citizen what to do, he better do it. They give orders and they're obeyed and I never knew how bad I wanted that. Zip into the Santa Rosa police training program, then I'm a cop, got three girlfriends, one black, one Asian, one white, cruising in a squad car all night long, kicking ass, busting heads, top of the world, man. One year into the deal I've got a sweet little wife and a six-week baby daughter. Two years in they put me on Narcotics and Vice, undercover. My job is to hang out in bars and party like Nero.

Can I do that? Hell, what do they think I've been doing every free minute anyhow? And will I buy drugs? Gee, okay, I'll give it a shot. And Howard, they say, listen, sometimes in the course of your duties you will have a line of coke laid out before you and in the course of your duties you'll just have to put your head down there and suck it up. It's part of the ride, okay Howard? Yeah, I say, part of the ride, and inside of six months I'm the biggest coke-head, the biggest dealer, and the crookedest cop in Northern California. I did armed robberies on dealers and drugstores up and down Highway 101. I had seven girlfriends and I was pimping every one. My sweet little wife divorced me and took my daughter and I never even noticed. The force gave me a thousand a month to buy coke in little bags and turn them in, and I had thirty thousand under my bed in a shoebox next to three or four kilos of coke the force would never see. I'd wake up in the afternoon and fare forth and wreak havoc. I murdered three guys I still claim the world is better off without, but I'm not the judge though, am I? But I sure thought I was. I took the lives of other human beings. I thought I was God. I looked in the mirror and said so— looked in the mirror and said, You are God. When God decided to prove me wrong, it all came down like a mountain of dogshit on my head. They rolled me up and socked me with so many charges, including at one point second degree murder, that if they stacked them up and ran me through I'd be doing time a hundred years past my natural death. I'm lying in jail and that cell is sucking the drugs and the fight and the soul right out me and giving it to God and God is squeezing it in his fingers, man, every last fiber of my soul in the almighty grip of the truth. And the truth is that everything I've done, every thought I've thought, every moment I've lived, is shit turned to dust and dust blown away. God, I said, fuck it, I'm not even gonna pray. Squeeze my guts till you get tired, that's all I want now, because at least it's real, it's true, it's got something to do with you. So then I think I died. I think I died in jail. My life itself just left me, and who you see before you now is someone else. So I wandered like a ghost through the court system and came out with a sentence of ten years. Did seven, one day at a time. Prayed every day and every night, but only one prayer: Squeeze till you get tired, Lord. Kill me, Lord, I don't care, as long as it's you who kills me. Just got outa Pelican Bay Prison eight days ago, and rehab is part of my parole. And nothing to show for thirty-six years on this earth. Except that God is closer to me than my next breath. And that's all I'll ever need or want. If you think I'm bullshitting, kiss my ass. My story is the amazing truth.

And me too, me too Brother John. My life is the amazing truth. Like Dad says "I put down one foot on the Road of Regret, and set out on my journey."

Just to sketch out the last four years—broke, lost, detox, homeless in Texas, shot in the ribs by a thirty-eight, mooching off the charity of Dad in Ukiah, detox again, run over (I think, I'm pretty sure, I can't remember) then shot again, and detox right now one more time again. Might've been one or two more detox trips and humiliating vacations at Dad's in there. Shot twice by the same guy, first he just grazed me when I was stealing his money and coke, second time he hunted me up and got me in the shoulder with a twenty-two derringer. Those twenty-two long-rifles HURT. I pity the folks who get the experience of the bigger calibers. Guarantee you a forty-four would take the arm right off a wiry sort of guy like me. More than once I've woke up with some medical professional saying, "You should be dead."

That's what it's gonna say on my gravestone—

"I Should Be Dead"

Your Brother In Christ,
Cass

STRANGLER

BOB

~~~~~

You hop into a car, race off in no particular direction, and blam, hit a power pole. Then it's off to jail. I remember a monstrous tangle of arms and legs and fists, with me at the bottom gouging at eyes and doing my utmost to mangle throats, but I arrived at the facility without a scratch or a bruise. I must have been easy to subdue. The following Monday I pled guilty to disturbing the peace and malicious mischief, reduced from felony vehicular theft and resisting arrest because—well, because all this occurs on another planet, the planet of Thanksgiving, 1967. I was eighteen and hadn't been in too much trouble. I was sentenced to forty-one days.

This was a county lockup, with its ground level devoted to the intake area and the offices and so on, and above that two levels for inmates. They put me on the lower tier among the rowdies and thugs. "Down here," the deputy promised me, "if you sleep late, you'll get your breakfast swiped." The air smelled like disinfectant and something else that was meant to be killed by disinfectant. The cells stayed open, and we were free to go in and out and congregate in the central area or stroll on the catwalk that girded the whole tier. This resulted in a lot of wandering around by as many as twenty men in denim pants and blue work shirts and rubber-soled canvas moccasins, a lot of pacing and stopping, and leaning and sitting, and getting up and pacing again. Most of us would have fit in perfectly in a psych ward. Many of us had already been there. I certainly had.

My cellmate was an older guy, late forties, with a bald head and a bowling-ball paunch, awaiting final disposition and sentencing. When I asked him sentencing for what, he told me, "something juicy." My second night there I overheard him talking to Donald Dundun, a boy about my age who had a habit of wandering the catwalk after lights-out, climbing on the bars and propping himself in cell doorways, stretching out his arms and legs, spread-eagling himself against the jambs and suspending himself in the air that way, and striking up idiotic conversations.

"My attorney already made the deal," I heard my cellmate tell Dundun. "I'm waiting for a date to go to court and plead out to twenty-five years. I'll get released the day I start drawing my Social Security."

"If you don't mind me asking," Dundun said, "what are you down for?"

"A misunderstanding with the wife."

"Ho ho! Maybe you can talk to mine!" Dundun danced away, apelike, and left us alone. He'd been caught leaving a third-story apartment by the window. He wanted to stay in shape for future high-elevation work.

The sounds of the cellblock faded, the last stray remarks, the thumping and coughing, and the bunkmate below me said, "You're the one they call Dink, right?"

"I have another name," I said. I lay in the top bunk, talking to the metal wall inches from my lips.

"Not in here you don't."

"What's yours?"

"Strangler Bob."

After a while I peeked over the bunk's edge and studied the face below me, now only a black oval, like a fencer's mask, and because I stared too long in the dark, the face began to boil and writhe.

The lower tier's standout resident was a young giant with a blond pompadour hairdo and an urchin's face— apple cheeks, fat forehead, happy blue eyes. The jailers called him Michael, but he referred to himself as Jocko, and the other prisoners did too. Jocko hustled around all day looking for somebody to listen to his opinions or, even better, arm-wrestle him. He said he'd been in county jails here and there a total of eighteen times, never for shorter than thirty days. He was not yet twenty-one. This time he'd been arrested for giving a man some well-deserved punishment in the dining area of the Howard Johnson's, which he described as the wrong kind of restaurant for that. Jocko knew all the deputies and staff around the jailhouse. He whispered to me that the sheriff's wife, who worked downstairs in the administrative office, had many times propositioned him. He lacked any ambition or strategy for crowning himself king of the cellblock, but he was nevertheless a star, and the lesser lights constellated around him. "Zit-suckers," he called them.

My first morning on the tier I did sleep through breakfast, and somebody did steal mine. After that I had no trouble rousing myself for the first meal, because other than the arrival of food we had nothing in our lives to look forward to, and the hunger we felt in that place was more ferocious than any infant's. Corn flakes for breakfast. Lunch: baloney on white. For dinner, one of the canned creations of Chef Boyardee, or, on lucky days, Dinty Moore. The most wonderful meals I've ever tasted.

After lunch most days Jocko organized a poker game that worked as follows: Hands of five-card draw would be dealt out and the draw accomplished, and the player with the highest hand got the privilege of slugging each of the others in the meat of his shoulder with such a smack it echoed around the metal environment. Only half a dozen prisoners took part. The rest of us could see that damage was being done. I kept to the farthest margins. I stood five-seven and weighed a hundred and twenty. As previously acknowledged, my nickname seemed to be "Dink"—not my choice.

One guy I never heard addressed by any name. He had no friends, never said hi or what's happening. He spent hours shuffling pigeon-toed around the catwalk, his skinny frame clenched and twisted by inner tension, throwing punches at the level of his waist as if pummeling an invisible child while whispering, "You sonofabitch fuckin *pig*, you fuckin *cop*," punctuating his speeches with explosive sound effects: "*shhssprgagahaBLAMMO!*" He had signal-flag ears, a chinless chin, scrunched forehead, his whole little face rushing out onto a really big nose, a regular beak—a face like a Mardi Gras mask. After his episodes he sat on the floor, rolling the back of his head from side to side against the steel rivets in the wall. The others watched him from a distance. But closely.

Early in December, on an afternoon proceeding no differently from any other afternoon as far as I could see, as usual very slowly unmasking itself as a damnation without end, Jocko screamed, "Fifty-two pickup!" and scattered the cards in the air and left the central area and disappeared into his cell. It was that moment in the day when time itself grew outrageously lopsided, getting farther and farther from lunch but somehow no closer to supper, and the bars became harder than iron, and you really felt locked up. The whole tier—common area, surrounding cells, and the catwalk enclosing everything—wasn't much larger than a basketball court, and anybody in there could have told you that if you went promenading on the catwalk, two hundred sixty steps would bring you back to where you started.

It was the moment for another nap, or for staring at the television. But this day the card players, weary and sore and absent a leader, turned their eyes toward the rest of us, and as soon as they landed on the nameless one, the crazy boy with the Mardi Gras face, we could feel a quickening, an igniting of certain materials that had been swimming around in our atmosphere all along.

The poker players were well into their twenties, a couple in their thirties, men awaiting trial for felonies or serving lengthy misdemeanor time. "Zit-suckers," Jocko called them, but today these six or seven men who played card games with their fists—including, today, Donald Dundun— were playing an even crazier game out on the catwalk, making themselves heard, hollering back and forth as they stalked the perimeter and took up positions on the outermost points of the compass, this handful of them commanding the whole cellblock and talking only about the kid, conspiring against his life while he watched TV and pretended not to hear.

"Come out on the catwalk." But he wouldn't come.

"Come on—it won't hurt."

Strangler Bob and I sat in our cell, side by side on his bunk. I didn't want to try and climb into mine because I was afraid to move.

"Somebody push the button!"

"Who said that?"

The boy was out of his chair now, and halfway to the button. "I didn't say it."

Dundun said, "Don't push it."

"I won't."

"Then who said push it?"

The big red button waited on the catwalk's wall between the electric cigarette lighter and the clanging door to the rest of the building, the same door through which our meals arrived, and in case of any trouble, this button would alert the deputies downstairs. But there was usually a sentry, one prisoner or another, posted beside the button to make sure it got no use.

Dundun made himself the sentry now. "Don't try it."

"I said I wasn't going to."

With his primitive hair and compact musculature, Dundun looked like a nasty little Neanderthal. "You'd better just face the situation."

The boy went back to the central area and sat down. He grabbed the seat of his chair with both hands and pretended to watch the TV bracketed to the corner of the room.

Dundun followed the boy and stood beside his chair. Together they watched a commercial for half a minute before Dundun reminded him, "What has to happen, has to happen."

"You don't seem too broken up about it," the boy said.

Jocko lost his cool. He pretty well combusted in his cell

and came out already burning alive. Leapt onto one of the two long dining tables and stood there looking at the ceiling, or the heavens, somewhat like a movie star in a climactic scene, and allowed a terrific energy to consume and become him.

Whether because he hated the idea of killing the crazy boy or because he thought they were taking too long to do it—well, he wasn't making it clear where he stood, except in the most general way: "I have HAD it!" Standing on the table, he lifted his arms and strained against invisible bars. He really was enormous, both muscular and overfed, looked fashioned from balloons, at least usually, but at this moment looked sculpted from quivering stone, his face plum-purple under the heap of yellow hair. "I have HAD it!" With a certain grace he stepped from tabletop, to chair, to floor. He marched around with vicious movements, crushing hallucinatory animals. His footsteps thundered on the catwalk. "I have HAD it. HAD it. HAD it."

No one knew what to make of these fireworks. Whatever its motive, Jocko's display had a quelling effect on the scene, if only because we all knew the guards were hearing it. Through the afternoon Jocko settled down by very slow degrees, and the next day he was his obnoxious, overly fraternal, scary former self again.

In the meantime, on this afternoon of the conspiracy against the kid with no name, the others went from blatantly murderous to ruminative and confused, and their plan for assassination climaxed in nothing more violent than sneaking up behind the boy on tiptoe and shooting rubber bands at the back of his head while he dedicated all his focus to *The Newlywed Game* and refused to flinch, refused to give them the satisfaction. The next morning the deputies called the boy away from his breakfast and moved him to the upper tier.

Rubber bands were permitted, yes. Books, magazines, candy, fruit—also cigarettes, if someone brought them to us, and if they didn't, then every two or three days the county provided each of its prisoners a packet of rough-cut tobacco called Prince Albert and a sheaf of cigarette papers— remember, 1967. Pets and children wandered loose in the streets. Respected citizens threw their litter anywhere. As for us lawbreakers, we lit our smokes on a pushbutton electric hotwire bolted to the cellblock wall.

Donald Dundun showed me how to roll a cigarette. Dundun came from the trailer courts, and I was middleclass gone crazy, but we passed the time together freely because we both had long hair and chased after any kind of intoxicating substance. Dundun, only nineteen, already displayed up and down both his arms the tattooed veins of a hope-to-die heroin addict. The same went for BD, a boy who arrived the week before Christmas. We knew him only as "BD". "My name cannot be pronounced, it can only be spelled." That was his dodge. I, on the other hand, didn't know the meaning of my own handle, "Dink." Some grouchy, puffy-eyed prisoner would walk by, look at me, and say, "Dink."

Dundun was short and muscled, I was short and puny, and BD was the tallest man in the jail, with a thick body that tapered up toward freakishly narrow shoulders. His head, however, was pretty large, with a curly brown mane. On the outs with his girlfriend, and consequently drunk, he'd decided to burgle a tavern. In the wee hours after closing time he'd climbed onto the roof with some tools to see if any way in could be found, stepped through the panes of a skylight, and landed flat on his face on the billiard table sixteen feet below; and the police woke him up.

BD didn't seem any worse for his plunge. It was understood he'd be collected soon and taken to the hospital and checked for invisible damage, but days passed, and it grew obvious he'd been forgotten.

Dundun, BD and I formed a congress and became the Three Musketeers—no hijinks or swashbuckling, just hour upon hour of pointless conversation, misshapen cigarettes, and lethargy.

BD told us he had a little brother, still in high school, who sold psychedelic drugs to his classmates. This brother came to visit BD and left him a hotrod magazine, one page of which he'd soaked in what he told BD was psilocybin, but was likelier just, BD figured, LSD plus some sort of large-animal veterinary tranquilizer. In any case: BD was most generous. He tore the page from the magazine, divided it into thirds, and shared one third with me and one with Donald Dundun, offering us this shredded contraband as a surprise on Christmas Eve. We gave away our suppers and choked down the paper on empty stomachs and waited to get lost. Jocko, the blond blimp, said, "God dang, your lips are black. And yours—and yours. Lemme see your tongue. What is the story? Did you catch the plague or something?"

"You got three extra suppers, so don't worry about it."— Jocko had eaten all three of our meals, plus his own.

BD came from the town of Oskaloosa about eighty miles away. A lot of disorderly characters rattled loose from there and ended up in Johnson County, often in the Johnson County jail. Prior to this encounter I hadn't known BD, but I was acquainted with his girlfriend Viola Percy, who lived right there in our town, in fact in the neighborhood of slum apartments where I myself had spent the summer—a formidable, desirable female in her late twenties, with a couple of tiny kids and a monthly stipend from the welfare department or Social Security, altogether an excellent woman to have in your corner. But Viola, whom BD described as both an angel and a devil, both the sickness and the cure, refused to visit him at the lockup, wouldn't even talk to him.

"The situation that got Viola Percy so mad at me," BD told us, "was that I fucked Chuckie Charleson's wife—but," he hastened to say, "only once, and practically by accident. I dropped by Chuckie's just to say hi, but he was shopping for shoes or something, and there's his wife all bored and itchy, and pretty soon we did the evil deed. And when I left the house, there was Chuckie sitting in his car out front drinking a beer and puffing on a Kool. Parked right behind my rig. Probably sitting there the whole time me and Janet are rolling around in his bed. And when I open the door to my truck, he flashes me the finger. And he's crying. Well, I feel sorry for Chuckie that he got married to a whore and a nympho, but shouldn't that be his own shit to carry? So I shut the door and drive off, and you figure that's the end of it. But no. *Charlie* has to go and tell *Viola*. God! It baffles me! Running to a guy's woman and saying, 'Boo-hoo, boo-hoo.' It's so sleazy, and so wrong, and so tiny. As a logical result, me and this guy Ed Peavey—do you know Ed Peavey?"—I had heard of him. Nobody else had.—"Okay, one guy's heard of Ed Peavey. Anyway, me and Ed Peavey, we dropped by Chuckie's, and we said to him, 'Chuckie, hey, even if you're a compulsive snitch and a certified eunuch, no hard feelings. We've got a case of beer, so let's be friends and go check out the river and sit in the shade and get drunk or something,' and we got him in my truck and took him maybe ten miles out of town on the Old Highway, and I stuck a gun in his ear and Ed wrestled off his pants and his undies and his shoes and socks and we drove off and left old Chuckie walking barefoot down the road like that toward town in just his teeshirt with his not very attractive ass hanging out. But . . . Viola. Viola will not forgive, and Viola will not forget. Hey. Is it snowing in here?"

By now the drug we'd swallowed should have been doing its work, but I felt no effect. When I asked the others about it, Dundun shook his head, but BD stared at me with eyes like two shiny mirrors and said, "All I know is this: Janet Charleson will pleasure any man alive."

"Does she pleasure animals too?"—Dundun wanted to know.

"I wouldn't doubt it."

"You mean Janet Charleson will do it with a goat? She'll let a billy goat hump her?"

"Like I say, I wouldn't doubt it." But BD frowned and withdrew into himself for a minute, and I bet he was wondering if inside this insatiable woman, Janet Charleson, he'd mixed his powers with those of a goat.

Dundun started climbing on the bars of the nearest cell. He'd slipped off his shoes and socks and now clung to the metal fretwork by his toes. BD said, "Is this shit hitting you like it's hitting me?" and Dundun said, "No, man, I'm just exercising."

Dundun's mental space, customarily empty, had been

invaded by an animal spirit. He gripped the bars with his left hand and foot, simultaneously stretching his right arm and leg straight out into the air, exactly in the style of a zoo monkey.

"Are you sure you're not feeling anything?" I asked him.

"I'm feeling all the way back to my roots. To the caves. To the apes." He turned his head and looked at us. His face was dark, but his eyeballs gave out sparks. He seemed to be positioned at the portal, bathed in prehistoric memories. He was summoning the ancient trees—their foliage was growing out of the walls of our prison, writhing and shrugging, hemming us in.

A voice laughed—"Hah!"—coming from my cellmate, Strangler Bob, who sat nearby on the catwalk's floor with his arms folded across his chest. Like all of us here, Strangler Bob knew how to sleep—from lights-out at ten until breakfast at seven, and a nap after breakfast, and a nap before supper—but this Christmas Eve he stayed up late and observed us with his dead soulless gaze.

BD, meanwhile, said, "I've never seen snow catching so many colors."

The potion wasn't evenly distributed on the page. BD had gotten most if not all of it, which was fair, but sad. The only effect I felt seemed to coalesce around the presence of Strangler Bob, who laughed again—"Hah!"—and when he had our attention said:

"It was nice, you know, it being just the two of us, me and the missus. We charcoaled a couple T-bone steaks and drank a bottle of imported Beaujolais red wine, and then I sort of killed her a little bit."

To demonstrate, he wrapped his fingers around his own neck while we musketeers studied him like something we'd come on in a magic forest.

Dundun clapped his hand on his forehead with a sound like a gunshot and said to the murderer, "You're the man who ate his wife!"

Strangler Bob said, "That was a false exaggeration. I did not eat my wife. What happened was, she kept a few chickens, and I ate one of those. I wrung my wife's neck, then I wrung a chicken's neck for my dinner, and then I boiled and ate the chicken."

"Wait a minute, Mr. Bob," BD said. "Can I get you to explain this to me? Do you mean to say you gobbled up a T-bone steak and red imported wine and all, and then you—you know, executed your wife—and *then* you had chicken? Like immediately after the crime, you were hungry again?"

"You sound like the prosecutor. He tried to make it an aggravating circumstance. It was just a chicken, a goddamn chicken." Strangler Bob's body had disappeared, his bald head floating—not just floating, but zooming through space. He said, "I have a message for you from God. Sooner or later, you'll all three end up doing murder." His finger materialized in front of him, pointing at each of us in turn—"Murderer. Murderer. Murderer"—pointing last at Dundun's nose. "You'll be the first."

"I don't care," Dundun said, and you could see it was true. He didn't care.

BD shivered wildly, and actually such a strong shudder ran through him that his curly hair flew around his head. "Can you really talk to God?"

At this I snorted like a pig. The idea of God disgusted me. I didn't believe. Everybody yacked and blabbered about cosmic spirituality and Hindu yogic chakras and Zen koans. Meanwhile, Asian babies fried in napalm. Right now I wished there was some way we could start this whole night over, leaving Strangler Bob out of it.

Immediately my wish came true when Dundun—excited, I guess, by this conversation with a murderer and by the prediction that he himself would murder someone—tendered a bizarre suggestion: "Let's bang the button."

While I stood in my tracks trying to decode these words, BD took them at their plain meaning and got himself in front of the button.

BD was tall, as I've said, and looked immovable. Dundun, however, swung hand over hand from the prehistoric vines and branches he'd summoned, and hung from the jungle's ceiling and pushed the red button with the heel of one bare foot. We heard a delicate sound—like an old-fashioned alarm clock in a 1930s movie tinkling distantly in the building's sleep. When a deputy arrived and called through the door—"What's going on in there?" BD said, "Nothing," but the deputy was only asking to pass the time while he got the key in the lock, and then three of them came in with batons and set about beating on the heads and bodies of anybody within reach. Murderer Bob went down in a ball on the floor the same as the Three Musketeers, and the deputies, when their arms were tired and they judged their duty properly exercised, said, "Don't touch that button no more tonight," and said, "That's right, Gentlemen," and also, "Or somebody's gonna get crippled."

We crawled off to our cells in a state of terror and bewilderment—though not Dundun, who seemed unaffected by the nightmare he himself had caused to explode in our faces, and strolled around the catwalk humming and scatting and fluttering his fingers along the bars. He didn't possess a complete brain.

I dragged my physical being, one big throbbing pulse, into an upper bunk I hoped was mine. During the festival of horrors my cellmate, Strangler Bob, had evaporated. Now here he was, reconstituted full-length in his bed. I stepped on his knee climbing into my bunk, and he didn't say anything. I expected some obscenities or at least a bitter "Merry Christmas," but not a peep. I studied him surreptitiously over the edge of the bunk, and soon I could see alien features forming on the face below me, Martian mouth, Andromedan eyes, staring back at me with evil curiosity. It made me feel weightless and dizzy when the mouth spoke to me with the voice of my grandmother: "Right now," Strangler Bob said, "you don't get it. You're too young." My grandmother's voice, the same aggrieved tone, the same sorrow and resignation.

I'll never go back to jail. I'll hang myself first.

BD must have felt the same about incarceration. About fifteen years after all this, in the early 1980s, he hanged himself in a holding cell in Florida. Looking at it one way, BD thereby committed a murder, so Strangler Bob's prediction for him came true. May he rest in peace.

. . . We saw Viola Percy one night.

The county jail and courthouse lay at the bottom of a hill on Court Street, and near the top of the hill, where Dubuque Street intersected, sometimes the relatives or friends—girlfriends, mostly, drunken girlfriends—of inmates came and stood, and waved and hooted, because we could get a pitiful glimpse of that particular spot from the cellblock's southeast corner, through the very last window. It was the night of New Year's Eve, and when a prisoner called us to the window, we all took turns looking at Viola, "my soul-mate and my heartbreak," BD called her, staged in the light of the streetlamp as at the far end of a long tunnel, dressed in a sort of go-go outfit or mini-raincoat made of plastic, with a white yachting cap and white boots halfway up her calves. A small, glittering rain would have perfected the picture, which was, all the same, as silent and remote and unattainable and sad as you could want. And very vague as to its meaning. Allowing him the sight of her in that lonely moment—what it signaled was left to BD to interpret. During my brief stay there, Viola never came to visit him.

While I was kept there I wondered if this place was some kind of intersection for souls. I don't know what to make of the fact that I've seen those same men many times throughout my life, repeatedly in dreams and sometimes in actuality—turning a corner on the street, gazing out the window of a passing train, or leaving a café just at the moment I glance up and recognize them, then disappearing out the door—and it makes me feel each person's universe is really very small, no bigger than a county jail, a collection of cells in which he encounters the same fellow prisoners over and over. BD and Dundun, in particular, turned up in my youth many times after this. I think they may have been not human beings, but wayward angels. I won't go into all the events they figured in, but I'll report this much about Dundun: A couple of years after we met in jail, he partnered up with the blond sociopathic giant Jocko, and together they robbed a notorious drug lord in Kansas City.

During the robbery Donald Dundun killed a bodyguard—giving truth to Strangler Bob's prediction.

You might go farther and say Strangler Bob's second sight proved out one hundred percent. The day after the Kansas City robbery, Dundun showed up at my door three hundred miles east of the scene of the crime, amazed at what he'd done and looking for a place to hide. We consumed a lot of his stolen heroin while he outwaited his pursuers in my little apartment, and when he felt safe and went away, he left me with a large quantity of the stuff, all mine, and over the course of the following month I became thoroughly addicted to heroin. I'd been addicted before, and I would be again, but this was the turning point. My fate was sabotaged. Thereafter, I was constantly drunk, treated myself as a garbage can for pharmaceuticals, and within a few years lost everything and became a wino on the street, drifting from city to city, sleeping in missions, eating at give-away programs . . . Very often I sold my blood to buy wine. Because I'd shared dirty needles with low companions, my blood was diseased. I can't estimate how many people must have died from it. When I die myself, BD and Dundun, the angels of the God I sneered at, will come to tally up my victims and tell me how many people I killed with my blood.

TRIUMPH OVER

THE GRAVE

~~~~~

Right now I'm eating bacon and eggs in a large restaurant in San Francisco. It's sunny, noisy, crowded—actually every table's occupied, and so I'm sitting at the bar that runs the room's entire length, and I'm facing the long wall-mirror, so that the restaurant behind me lies spread out before me, and I'm free to stare at everyone with impunity, from behind my back, so to speak, while little yelps and laughs from their chopped-up conversations rain down around me. I notice a woman behind me—as I face her reflection— sharing breakfast at a table with her friends, and there's something very familiar about her . . . Okay, I've realized, after staring at her a bit, quite without her knowledge, that her face looks very much like the face of a friend of mine who lives in Boston—Nan, Robert's wife. I don't mean it's Nan. Nan in Boston is a natural redhead, whereas this one's a brunette, and somewhat younger, but there's so much of Nan in the way this woman moves her mouth, and something about her fingers—her manner of gesturing with them as she speaks, as if she's ridding them of dust, precisely as Nan does—that I wonder if the two might be sisters, or cousins, and the idea isn't far-fetched, because I know Nan in Boston actually comes from San Francisco, and she has family here.

An impulse: I think I'll call Nan and Robert. They're in my phone (odd expression). I'm gonna call . . .

Okay. I just called Robert's number. Immediately someone answered and Nan's voice cried, "Randy!" "No, I'm not Randy"—and I tell her it's me. "I have to get off the phone," Nan says, "there's a family emergency. It's awful, it's awful, because Robert . . ." As in a film, she breaks down sobbing after the name. I know what that means in a film. "Is Robert all right?" "No! No! He's—" and more sobbing. "Nan, what happened? Tell me what happened." "He had a heart attack this morning. His heart just stopped. They couldn't save him. He's dead!" I can't accept this statement. I ask her why she would say such a thing. She tells me again: Robert's dead. "I can't talk now," she says. "I've got a lot of people to call. I have to call my sister, all my family in San Francisco, because they loved him so dearly. I have to get off the line," and she did.

I put away my phone and managed to write down that much of the conversation in this journal, on this very page, before my hand started shaking so badly I had to stop. I imagined Nan's fingers shaking too, touching the face of her own cellphone, calling her loved ones with the unbelievable news of a sudden death. I rotated my barstool, turned away from my half-eaten meal, and stared out over the crowd.

There's the brown-haired woman who so resembles red-

headed Nan. She stops eating, sets down her fork, rum-
mages in her purse—takes out her cellphone. She places it
against her ear and says hello . . .

—I left my breakfast unfinished and went back to the
nearby hospital, where I'd dropped a friend of mine for
some tests. We called him Link, shortened from Linkewits.
For many weeks now I'd been living with Link in his home,
acting as his chauffeur and appointments clerk and often
as his nurse. Link was dying, but he didn't like to admit it.
Weak and sick, down to skin and bones, he spent whole
days describing to me his plans for the renovation of his
house, which was falling apart and full of trash. He couldn't
manage much more than to get up once or twice a day to
use the bathroom or heat some milk and instant oatmeal
in his microwave, could hardly turn the pages of a book,
lay unconscious as many as twenty hours at a stretch, but
he was charting a long future. Other days he embraced
the truth, made decisions about his property, instructed
me as to his funeral, recalled his escapades, spoke of
long-departed friends, considered his regrets, pondered his
odds—wondered whether experience continues, somehow,
after the heart stops. These days Link left his house only to
be driven to medical appointments in San Francisco, Santa
Rosa, Petaluma—that's where I came in. Now, while I sat in
a waiting room and the technicians in Radiology put him
under scrutiny, making sure of what they already knew, I

took out a pen and my notebook and finished jotting a quick account of my recent trip to the restaurant and my sighting of the woman I believed to be Nan's sister. I've reproduced it verbatim in the first few paragraphs above.

Writing. It's easy work. The equipment isn't expensive, and you can pursue this occupation anywhere. You make your own hours, mess around the house in your pajamas, listening to jazz recordings and sipping coffee while another day makes its escape. You don't have to be high-functioning or even, for the most part, functioning at all. If I could drink liquor without being drunk all the time, I'd certainly drink enough to be drunk half the time, and production wouldn't suffer. Bouts of poverty come along, anxiety, shocking debt, but nothing lasts forever. I've gone from rags to riches and back again, and more than once. Whatever happens to you, you put it on a page, work it into a shape, cast it in a light. It's not much different, really, from filming a parade of clouds across the sky and calling it a movie—although it has to be admitted that the clouds can descend, take you up, carry you to all kinds of places, some of them terrible, and you don't get back where you came from for years and years.

Some of my peers believe I'm famous. Most of my peers have never heard of me. But it's nice to think you have a skill, you can produce an effect. I once entertained some children with a ghost story, and one of them fainted.

I'll write a story for you right now. We'll call this story "The Examination of my Right Knee." It happened a long time ago, when I was twenty or twenty-one. Since shortly after my fifteenth birthday, my right knee had been tricky— locking into place sometimes when I bent my leg, and staying that way until I found just the combination of position and movement that would set the joint free again. For years I'd tried ignoring the problem, but it had only gotten worse, and so, during my junior year as an undergraduate, I reported it to the experts at the university hospital. An X-ray indicated torn cartilage. The head of Orthopedics himself was going to take a closer look, and I waited in a hallway outside his door in a green robe and paper slippers.

Almost nothing went on in this hallway. Now and then a medical person in green or white padded by. After a while, about fifty feet along the corridor, a middle-aged man in a dark business suit started talking into a wall-mounted payphone. For most of the conversation his back was turned to me, but at one point he pivoted with a certain frustrated energy, and a few of his words reached my ears: "I was never an animal lover."

At that moment the door I was waiting for opened, and an orderly in white asked me to come in.

I followed this orderly not into a tiny examination room, but instead onto a brightly lit stage in an auditorium filled with hundreds of people—medical students, as best I could make out against the glare illuminating me. Nobody had warned me I'd be exhibited. In the center of the stage, under blinding lamps of the kind portrait photographers use, the orderly helped me onto a gurney and posed me on my back like a calendar girl, the knee raised, the robe parted, my bare leg displayed.

In those days I took recreational drugs at every opportunity, and about an hour earlier, as a way of preparing for this experience, or maybe just by coincidence, I'd ingested a lot of LSD, which had the effect of focusing my awareness more acutely on the pain in the knee, at the same time unmasking pain, in itself, as something cosmically funny, as well as revealing the overwhelming, eternal vitality of the universe, especially of the dark, surrounding audience, who breathed and sighed in unison, like one huge creature.

The head of Orthopedics approached me. He was either a large, almost gigantic person, or a person who only seemed gigantic under the circumstances. He gripped my flesh with his seething monster-hands and delivered a lecture while he manipulated my lower leg and fondled the joint in preparation, I felt pretty sure, of eating me. "Now you'll see how the disfigured cartilage causes the joint to seize," he said, but he couldn't produce the effect, and went on straightening and bending the leg at the knee and talking jibber-jabber. Meanwhile, I observed that the Great Void of Extinction was swallowing the whole of reality at an impossible rate of speed, and yet nothing could overcome our continual birthing into the present.

The Colossus of Orthopedics clamped my thigh with one hand and my ankle with the other and cranked the lower leg around gently, then not so gently, saying, "Sometimes it takes a bit of fiddling." Still the knee didn't lock. Before this vast audience of his students, he pronounced me a faker. "There's no condition here requiring any treatment at all," he said. He pointed at me with a finger that communicated billions of accusations simultaneously. "A lot of these young men are out to fool the medical establishment, because they don't want to get drafted."

It was easy enough for me to get the knee to lock. I just had to bend my leg so the knee was raised and turn my foot forty-five degrees to the right. The noise it made when it locked was disgusting—a horrid, gulping thunk. The sound came from the pre-chaotic depths, where good and evil were one thing.

"Ah—you see,"—the mammoth said to his compatriot, the darkness. "Now you see!" I understood this to mean he was about to turn me invisible, and soon after that he'd amuse the students by making me explode. Then I grasped that he was an orthopedic specialist who, having failed to get the knee locked until I'd done it for him, was now going to show his students how to unlock it again. But he couldn't do that either. After a lot of huffing and puffing and mumbo jumbo, he collapsed in his inwardmost self and prayed unto the darkness for help, and his prayer was heard.

The darkness furnished forth the Unlocker, who seemed a loving emanation, then a mysterious becoming, then a glorious actuality, and at last a sort of porky med student, who leapt onto my knee hind-end-first, as you'd do if you wanted to shut a bulging suitcase. Again the great sound, the Gulp of God, and my bones were restored, and with an infinitude of applause too wonderful for human ears, Creation burst its beginnings. The hero took my hand, and, having been exhibited before the All, having been lain out, and locked, and unlocked, at his touch I was able to rise, and walk.

In the quiet hallway I sat down alone. The man who'd been talking on the payphone was still there, still talking, as if nothing had ever happened. I strained to hear his magical words. For what it's worth, I'll repeat them here. He said: "Your dog. Your dog. Your dog. You were a fool to leave your dog with me."

You're writing about one thing, next second about something else—things medical—things literary—things ghostly—and onto the empty page steps a novelist named Darcy Miller. Among other books, Darcy wrote one called *Ever the Wrong Man*, which became a movie in 1982—Darcy also wrote the screenplay. He published as D. Hale Miller. Incidentally, I'm aware it's the convention in these semi-

autobiographical tales—these pseudo-fictional memoirs—
to disguise people's names, but I haven't done that . . . Has
thinking of Link, my sick friend, brought Darcy to mind?
The two men were quite similar, each ending up alone in
his sixties, resigned and self-sufficient, each one living, so
to speak, as his own widow. And then the ebbing of self-
sufficiency, the gradual decline—gradual in Link's case, and
in Darcy's quite a bit swifter.

I made Darcy's acquaintance in the year 2000 in Austin,
Texas, where he lived in an old house on an abandoned
ranch. That sounds glummer than it was. Darcy had come
there for a four-month period at the invitation of the University of Texas, which owned the ranch and maintained the
premises, and he got a stipend, probably a meager one, but
anyway he had a roof over his head, and he wasn't broke. I
happened to be teaching a writing course at the university
that same semester, and one day in early spring I led my
dozen graduate students, in three cars, out to the old place
to hold our class there as Darcy's guests. We headed west
out of Austin, first onto backcountry roads and then off the
paved byways entirely, crossing two large ranches on a
miles-long dirt easement and meeting a series of widely
separated gates we had to unlock and open (I'd been given
the combinations on a slip of paper) and shut and lock behind us. By the odometer we traveled three dozen miles, no
more, and on the map we moved well short of one-half de-

gree westward in longitude, but Austin is situated such that this brief journey took us out of the lush southeastern part of Texas and into the scrubby semidesert of the state's southwestern half, where you need ten acres of this mean, miserly grass, an old cowboy once told me, to keep one head of cattle from starving; fording with a splash and gurgle a tiny creek within sight of the house and the stables behind it, passing under creekside cottonwoods and shaggy willows, planted long ago for windbreaks and now grown monumentally large, and swinging around Darcy's car, a well used fake-luxury Chrysler parked just across the creek and still some distance from the house, as if it had made it very nearly the whole way and then given up.

Darcy seemed like that too, a little. He had tousled reddish hair and puffy features and looked something like a child snatched from a nap. He had ice-blue, very shiny, bloodshot eyes, and on his cheeks and across his nose the burst capillaries once known as "gin blossoms." We gathered behind the house on a patio of broken flagstones—the interior was a bit too small for entertaining. Darcy served us iced tea poured from two large pitchers into old canning jars, and that's what he drank, too, as he described for us the stages, a better word is paroxysms, by which his first novel had become a successful movie more than a decade after its publication. First the producers added years to the hero's age and signed John Wayne; some weeks into the development process, however, John Wayne died. They dialed back the hero's age and cast Rip Torn, Darcy told our class as we sat around a crude wooden table in the willows' shade, but Rip Torn got arrested, not for the first time, or the last, and then an actor named Curt Wellson turned up, absolutely perfect for the role, the success of the project so assured by this young man's unprecedented talent that he held out for an unprecedented fee for his services, lost his chance, and was never heard of again. Clint Eastwood liked it, and said so for nearly two years before negotiations hit a wall. In a fit of silliness, pure folly, the producers took an offer to Paul Newman. Newman accepted. The film was shot, cut, and distributed, and it did all right for everybody involved.

Nothing much had happened since then to D. Hale Miller, at least not in the eyes of my students, that was plain, although for better than thirty years he'd survived, and occasionally thrived, as a writer—of unproduced scripts, uncollected magazine articles, and two more novels after *Ever the Wrong Man*. All three books had gone out of print.

Throughout our visit Darcy seemed in good spirits and in command of himself. He dealt generously with the works under discussion, though he addressed the students—men and women in their mid-twenties—as "you children." He wore baggy Wrangler jeans, a light checked short-sleeved

shirt, and flip-flop zoris, their yellow straps gripping myth-
ically horrible feet—knobby, veiny, with toenails like tal-
ons. I shouldn't have been staring at them, but shortly into
the visit I found I didn't like my students' attitude and
wished we hadn't come here, and I focused on such irrelevant details as Darcy's feet in order to cancel out the rest,
the physical vastness of empty Texas, the heartfelt, demor-
alized lowing of distant cattle, the buzzards hanging in the
sky, all of that, and in particular the young writers around
the table, attentive, encouraging, yet thoroughly dismis-
sive. They could see Darcy's exile but not his battered no-
bility. The waves had rolled him half-alive onto foreign
sands, and now he was sipping his tea, commenting on our
attempted stories, and slowly shifting the position of his left
elbow to dislodge a fly that kept landing on it. I'm not sure
how the day ended and I don't remember the trip back into
Austin, but I recall stopping at a video rental shop later that
night, or on a night soon after, looking for a copy of *Ever
the Wrong Man.* The store's catalog listed the title, but it
was missing from the shelves.

   That was my first encounter with Darcy Miller. The next
one came five or six weeks later, after I got a completely
unexpected message at work: I'd received a phone call from
the writer Gerald Sizemore, G. H. Sizemore on his books
and Jerry to his acquaintances. As soon as I got his message

I called him back, and after a quick hello he went right to the point: "I want you to go out and see Darcy Miller. I'm worried about him."

I'd never met Gerald Sizemore, and we'd never even corresponded, but it didn't surprise me that I was known to him and that he felt, moreover, that he could ask of me just about any favor, because some years earlier I'd written an introduction for the twentieth anniversary edition of his first novel, *The Reason I'm Lost*, published in 1972 and now, as I'd argued in my preface for it, an American classic. Like Darcy Miller, Sizemore had published three books but had lived mainly as a screenwriter, with fair success; had written many scripts, including one he co-authored in the early 1970s with, as he told me now, Darcy Miller: a romantic romp starring Peter Fonda and Shelley Duvall that had been filmed in its entirety but never actually finished—a union strike interfered with post-production; the studio changed hands and the new owners filed for Chapter Eleven; in the middle of it all the chief cinematographer ran away to Mexico with the director's wife; and so on—and therefore never distributed. I'd been completely unaware of Gerald Sizemore's connection with Darcy Miller. Jerry, as he invited me to call him, described his and Darcy's alliance as reaching back into their twenties, and the plot, such as it was, of *The Reason I'm Lost* paralleled the course of their friendship as young writers learning their craft in the San Francisco scene of the early 1960s. Later, in the 1970s, after the hungry years, Darcy and Jerry shared their successes together—books coming out, a movie being made, money coming in. That was back when writers were still sort of important and, as with athletes, "promise" draped even the unproven ones with a certain glamor. I'll offer myself as an example: I was, in those days, eighteen and nineteen and twenty years old, and newspapers in Chicago and Des Moines ran articles about me because I was someday going to be a writer—I wasn't one yet, I was just going to be, and on the strength of this expectation I was invited to ladies' clubs throughout the Midwest to read from the couple of dozen existing pages of my work and answer questions from club members, and there were two or three of these mid-western, middle-aged, formerly good-looking women I could probably have seduced (though I lacked magnetism and still had acne) because in 1972 it would have been an adventure to be seduced by a figure of future literary prominence, and later watch him rise. Meanwhile, Darcy and Jerry were having the time of their lives as figures of current literary prominence, adventuring with currently good-looking women, mostly in Darcy's big home by the Pacific in Humboldt County, California. That would have been around the moment of my fame as a medical cu-

riosity at the University Hospital—I told you about that—
which is maybe why that old college memory surfaced a bit
ago, and there's the fresher memory, too, of my recent experience taking care of my close friend Link; and those two
memories together led me to recollect Darcy and . . . but
we've already mentioned the conjoining of these memories,
so what's the fuss? I'll get on with it. Jerry was worried
about his old friend. "I don't know what's going on out
there," he said, "at that ranch, or farm, or—"

"The Campesino Place."

"So it's a place?"

"In Texas, a ranch would be thousands of acres. A couple hundred is just a place."

"Darcy doesn't answer his phone, and his message ma-
chine is full—anyway it drills your ear with this endless,
screaming beep, and then it hangs up, and I assume that
means it's full—and for more than a week now I can't get a
rise out of the guy. The lady at the Writing Center—Mrs.—"

"Mrs. Exroy—"

"Mrs. Exroy. Interesting name. She says you saw Darcy
a couple months ago. Did he seem all right?"

"He seemed fine to me. I mean, he's how old—?"

"He's sixty-seven. The thing is, before he stopped an-
swering the phone, he called me several days in a row to
bitch and complain about his brother. Says his brother and

his sister-in-law turned up last month, and he can't make them leave. They're messing up the kitchen, drinking his liquor, getting in his way."

"So maybe it's not such a concern, then, if he's got family there—"

"No. I'm very concerned."

"But if his brother's there—"

"His brother's been dead for ten years."

This was the kind of moment when, in the distant past, I'd put a cigarette between my lips and light up and take a drag—but I don't smoke now—in order not to seem stupefied.

"They're both deceased. The sister-in-law died more recently."

I said, "Ah-hah."

"She died in '95. I went to both their funerals."

I said again ah-hah.

"So Darcy Miller's hanging around with a couple of ghosts," Jerry said, "or claims to be."

I promised him I'd get out there and have a look.

As soon as we'd said goodbye, I tried Darcy's number without even putting down the receiver. Following several ring tones came a long, long beep, and the connection ended. Only then did I place the receiver in its cradle on my desk. I was in my office at the Writers' Center, which looked down, on the window side, at the four lanes of Keaton Street

and, through the doorway on my left, at the grandly pro-
portioned mesquite table around which we gathered our
seminars. The conference room itself was a modest space
lined with shelves of books, once the study of the Texas
author Benjamin Franklin Brewer and still containing the
old pale green—springtime green—leather reclining chair
in which Brewer sat and read, and made his notes, and, one
day, stretched out and died. The building had formerly
been Brewer's home. At the moment, around four on a Friday afternoon, I had the upper floor to myself—three offices, a bathroom (with tub) and the conference room.
Sometimes, when alone up here like this and trapped in a
melancholy mood, I sat in the recliner and operated its an-
tique mechanism and lay back and tried to imagine the
going out of Benjamin Franklin Brewer's last breath. Under
the influence of these surroundings, I thought I'd better go
right now and look in on Darcy Miller.

Downstairs I got the combinations for the gate locks
from the center's administrative assistant—this was Mrs.
Exroy, a plump, diligently pleasant older southern widow
who liked to stand on the back porch and smoke cigarettes
while gazing at the little ravine and the creek out back of
the building, as if the trickle of water carried her thoughts
away. She always brought to my mind the phrase "sweet
sorrow."

I got on the road not long after 4 p.m. Right away the

traffic ensnarled me, if that's a word, and it was well past five by the time I came to the dirt roads. It seemed to me I'd reach Darcy's home with plenty of daylight left, but I wasn't sure of any daylight coming back; to save troubling with the combinations later in the dark I left the gate locks open and dangling, a scandalous breach of cowboy etiquette, but one I expected to go unnoticed because from horizon to horizon, as I realized now, making the trip this time without passengers to divert me, not a single shelter was visible, and I saw nothing, really, other than the gates and the miles of smooth wire fencing, to suggest that anybody cared what went on here or even knew of the existence of this place. I passed a few longhorn steers, or bulls, or cows, I couldn't have said which, a very few, each standing all alone beneath the burden of a pair of horns that reach, from tip to tip, "up to seven feet," according to absolutely every article I've ever seen about these animals; they wear out the phrase. Here in the Americas we trace the longhorn line back to the livestock cargo of Columbus's second expedition to the New World, and farther back, of course, in the Old World, to a scattered population of eighty or so wild aurochs domesticated in the Middle East more than ten thousand years ago, the forebears of all the cattle living now under human dominion. In 1917 the University of Texas adopted as its mascot a longhorn steer named "Bevo." As far as I've been able to determine, the two syllables mean nothing and may derive from the word "beef." In 2004, a successor Bevo—Bevo the Fourteenth—attended George W. Bush's presidential inauguration in Washington, D.C.

At the fourth gate, the final one, I knelt before the lock while my Subaru idled behind me. Way up the straight road I could make out the willows and cottonwoods surrounding Darcy's house, and looking at my destination and the half mile of empty ground between us, I was overwhelmed by a clear, complete appreciation of the physical distance behind me, as if I'd walked the twenty-some-odd miles rather than driven across the landscape in a car. A few minutes later, when I came in sight of the creek, I witnessed a school of vultures, the huge redheaded scavengers called in these parts turkey buzzards, nine or ten of them, eleven, I couldn't count, orbiting above the house on spiral currents. I stopped my car and watched. The truth is I was afraid to go any farther—no word from the house's occupant for many days, and now these circling creatures, taken everywhere as omens of death because they forage by smell, scouting the thermal drafts that carry them for any whiff of ethyl mercaptan, the first in the series of compounds propagated by carnal putrefaction and one recognizable to many of us, I've since learned, as the agent added to natural gas in order to make it stink. Floating above the house, the buzzards looked no more substantial than burning pages, gliding very gradually downward but then, after no perceptible alteration or adjustment, gliding upward, mounting high enough to seem no longer invested in the scene below, wherein none of the things—Darcy's car, the house, the row of six whitewashed stables roofed with black asphalt shingles—seemed out of the ordinary, but neither did anything seem to move. Suddenly I felt as if the view before me had shrunk to the size of a tabletop. To the east, hundreds of meters beyond the buildings, the buzzards' shadows raced over the scrubby tangles of a mesquite chaparral like the shadows of a mobile in a child's bedroom. I engaged the accelerator and moved forward—shrinking now, myself, in order to enter among the miniatures and the toys.

As I banged on the house's door, the buzzards twenty and thirty feet above me showed no reaction and continued their rondelle. I heard nothing from inside, peeked in the living room window—saw nobody—banged some more—still nothing—and was reaching out my hand to test the knob when the door came open and Darcy Miller stood before me. He wore a striped lab coat, and he was barefoot, if I recall, although it's hard to recall, because the lab coat was hanging open, and beneath it Darcy seemed to be completely naked, and I didn't know where to look. So I didn't look anywhere.

Darcy made no greeting, only studied me until I reintroduced myself and asked him if he was doing okay. He said, "Perfectly okay."

"Jerry Sizemore asked me to come out because he can't get you on the phone. What have you been doing with yourself out here?"

"Thangdoodlin'."

"Thangdoodlin'?"

He turned away and sat down on the couch without explaining the term—also, I'm afraid, without closing his robe—and I sat down beside him. I feel a natural impulse here, having just entered Darcy's personal field, to stop and describe his face—the bloodshot, ice-blue eyes, the fishnet grapestains over his nose and cheeks—or his horny feet, or his crop of wispy hair once probably reddish, now translucent—but, as I say, I was blinded by my embarrassment, and I can now offer only the additional details that Darcy smelled like booze and that I heard the faint whistle of breath in his nose just the way I heard the breathing of grownups through their hairy, cavernous nostrils when I was a child. For a little bit, that was the only sound in the house, the whistling of Darcy's nose . . . He said, "I think I can make you some tea. Is that what you want?"

"First," I said, "can we talk a little about what's going on with you? Jerry's worried, I'm worried—"

"What's got you so worried?"

I felt lost. "Well, I mean, for one thing, you've got your robe open there, and your package is just—hanging out."

The lab coat closed with metal snaps. He fumbled with a couple to get it shut. "Maybe I'm expecting a young lady."

(Now I noticed faint freckles on the backs of his hands and noted how pale were the little hairs. His lips were gray and blue, as if he were cold.)

"Jerry thinks you might be losing it out here."

"Losing what?"

"Your mind."

"Who wouldn't? Let's have a cup."

He led me into a short passageway with the linoleum-era kitchen on the left, the door to a "spare room" across from it on the right, and the master bedroom and bath at the end. We sat at the wobbly Formica table in the kitchen while Darcy, with a fastidiousness arising, I would guess, from a sense his competence was under review, got out all the stuff and brewed us a pot of Lipton's tea. I went right to the subject of the visitors—the ghosts—and he said, "No, they're not ghosts. It's them. They're alive."

"Even though they're both dead and buried."

"Yeah."

"But Darcy, don't you think that's—crazy?"

"Certainly! It's the craziest thing ever. Yesterday I saw

Ovid walking out there by the stables," Darcy said, much to my confusion, until I realized Ovid must be the brother, "and we sat over there on that big old cottonwood stump, side by side, and talked."

"Can I ask what you were talking about?"

"Nothing too specific. Just this and that."

"Did you ask Ovid to explain his presence? Did you remind him he's supposed to be dead?"

"No! What would you think if I said to you right now— Hey, man, you're supposed to be dead?"

"I don't know."

"How would that fit into any reasonable or polite conversation?"

"I don't know."

"Neither do I."

"Darcy, when was the last time you had a checkup?"

"Oh. Hell. A checkup?"

"Do you have a doctor here in Austin?"

"No. But I have a nurse in San Francisco."

"You have a nurse? What does that mean, you have a nurse?"

"She's more of a girlfriend. But she's a nurse at Cal Pacific. She's a Native American. She's Pomo Indian."

"Do you two talk on the phone?"

"Sure. She's very tuned in to this sort of business, the

ethereal waves and the currents, or anyway she says she is—the spirits and the haunts and the songs of the mother Earth."

"So, then, you've told her about all this—about your dead brother and dead sister-in-law visiting you?"

"Yeah."

"And what does she say?"

"She says it means I'm dying."

Well, I could see that as one possibility. But not as a result of illness, only as the inevitable outworking of the days of D. Hale Miller, and it was a lot like the destiny I'd pictured for myself when I was a criminally silly youth: a washed-up writer with books and movies and affairs and divorces behind him and nothing to show for it now, eking out a few last years—drinking, sinking. Of course in my youth it had seemed romantic because it was just a picture. It didn't have an odor. It didn't smell like urine and alcoholic vomit. And the way I'd been rushing at it, if I'd continued toward that kind of end it would have come a lot sooner, in my twenties, if I had to guess, preceded by not much.

"It doesn't look like your car has moved."

"It works fine, but I don't like to drive it."

"How do you get supplies?"

"They bring stuff. Bess and Ovid. They bring everything."

We drank our tea, which wasn't bad. Darcy had puffy red hands, the flesh extremely wrinkled, and as I studied his fingers they began to look like eight dancer's legs clothed in droopy stockings of flesh, marching and kicking around the tabletop in front of him, pushing his china cup and saucer around, leaping onto and wrestling with a crisp clean orange-and-white University of Texas baseball cap, which he never placed on his head. My plunge into despair felt vividly physical. If I'd closed my eyes I'd have been sure a colossal savage was dragging my chair through the floor and down through mile after mile of the dirt below. If I'd had control of my senses, my awareness, which I did not, I'd have noticed the afternoon had turned toward evening, and I'd have looked around for a light switch. We sat in a deepening gloom.

"Darcy, these visitors, Bess and Ovid—where are they right now?"

One of his fingers fluttered upward from the table, dragging the rest of the hand with it, to point across the hallway. He said, "Look"—and I looked, terrified my gaze might follow this indication right into the faces of two ghosts, but he concluded—"in that room." He meant the spare room.

I stood up and entered the hallway. I won't pretend I had any thoughts at all, only sensations, a coppery taste in my mouth, a pervading weakness, mostly in the legs, a buzzing around my temples and behind my eyes. I put my hand on the door's old-fashioned tongue latch, but for several seconds I couldn't operate my own fingers. I remembered this spare room from my first visit to the U of Texas a few years earlier, long before Darcy ever came there. The room lay in the center of the house and may originally have been some sort of pantry, I don't know. It lacked windows and amounted to a twelve-by-twelve-foot box constructed of yellowing whitewashed planks. Over the years the seams between the planks had opened to finger-wide gaps which had been stopped with spray-foam insulation that congealed in grotesque, snotty rivulets reminiscent of limestone cave formations, hard to look at but impermeable to scorpions. Mrs. Exroy, who'd given me the tour, had told me about the scorpions and said the foam insulation was there to keep them out—that is, to imprison them in the darkness behind the walls—while an image of them poured through the cracks into the impressionable mind, teeming there with their stinger-tipped venom sacs waving at the ends of their segmented tails and their pincers clacking like castanets on the ends of their loathsome pedipalps. I now felt convinced that something real, something horrid was happening to this man in this house, and the bizarre shrinking sensation I'd experienced earlier was now explained (despite remaining utterly mysterious) as the result of my having passed through a succession of ever smaller perimeters whose entries I'd breached as if in my sleep, blind to their significance—each of the four gates; then the creek; then the constellation of the vultures at this moment still wheeling above the roof; and finally the bounds of the house itself—toward the pair of entities, Bess and Ovid, waiting behind this door.

I depressed the latch and pushed the door wide, and the twilight from the hallway fell across the only things in the space, a single-size metal bedframe and its bare, grayed, filthy mattress—only these two objects, twisted invisibly by the several concentric gales of power whirling around them for a radius of twenty miles. A bit of light touched the walls, enough to reveal that they were undisturbed, and still disturbing. The disfiguring goop had the sandy pallor and plasticine shine of a scorpion's exoskeleton, so that to me it appeared multiple tons of scorpions were being mashed against the wall's other side and extruding from the cracks. I shut the door fast, like a frightened child.

To be clear, I hadn't seen any scorpions or any people or any ghosts.

I joined Darcy in the kitchen. Fear had eaten up my patience. Sitting down I was rough with my chair. "Somebody's bullshitting somebody."

"Maybe they're on a walk."

"Where did these visitors come from in the first place? The underworld?"

"Oklahoma."

"How'd they get here, Darcy? Where's their car?"

"I don't know. In one of the stables, maybe."

"I can look right out this window and tell you the stables are empty."

"Or maybe they're on a drive."

"When was the last time you saw these two people?"

"I don't know—an hour ago?"

I think the change in my manner sobered Darcy. He became instantly cooperative and peered into my face and nodded his head as we agreed that come Monday I'd make calls and get him the soonest possible date with a doctor. More disturbing than the idea he was trafficking with hallucinations was his blank-faced toleration of the circumstance. This weird placidity seemed to be his chief symptom—that, and failing to shut his robe—but symptomizing what?

Before saying goodbye I went through the house and turned on all the lights, leaving the spare room closed and dark. For this operation I got Darcy's permission first, naturally, and a bright interior seemed to cheer him up. When we shook hands on parting, he gripped mine firmly and cracked it like a whip.

I drove from gate to gate across the pastureland with the sunset on my left. Along the way I passed a scene of carnage: half a dozen redheaded vultures on the ground, beleaguering a carcass too small to be seen in their midst.

When we catch sight of one of these birds balanced and steering on the currents, its five-pound body effortlessly carried by the six-foot span of its wings and therefore not quite constituting a material fact, the earthbound soul forgets itself and follows after, suddenly airborne, but when they're down here with the rest of us, desecrating a corpse, brandishing their wings like the overlong arms of chimpanzees, bouncing on the dead thing, tearing at it, their nude red heads looking imbecilically minuscule and also, to a degree, obscene—isn't it sad? By the way, the ones circling above the house were gone by the time I left the place, and no explanation for them has ever suggested itself. I'd left after only an hour's visit, and had an hour of daylight before the evening overtook me on the freeway into Austin and bathed the city in a purple dusk in which the lights floated and we assume everyone is happy.

That year, the year 2000, our small family—mom and dad, son and daughter, dog and cat—had wintered comfortably in Austin, and now the others had flown north to our home in Idaho and left me, during Finals Week, on my own and accountable to nobody for my evenings. After that baffling afternoon at Darcy's I drove back to the Writers' Center, where I could park, and walked through the muggy southern evening to the arid oasis of the University's undergraduate library. At a table in an alcove on the third floor I opened a blue-bound, musty copy of *The Reason I'm Lost* and read about Gabe Smith and Danny Osgood, two San Francisco jazz men who live far from the recording studios and deep in the sorrow and glory of artistic struggle.

I turned first to a five-page passage late in the book—an argument between Osgood and his girlfriend Maureen, the first bit of dialogue I'd ever scrutinized for its ups and downs, the turns and turns-about, the strategies of the combatants. These long years later I could still recite the lines along with the characters, yet they sounded new.

I looked back at the novel's opening paragraph, and by midnight I'd read the whole thing again and found myself just as moved as I'd been the first time—the first dozen times—every time. *The Reason I'm Lost* wasn't just an exercise in exemplary prose. Ultimately this book, and my envy of it, were about the friendship between Danny Osgood and Gabriel Smith. A private and a corporal, they meet as members of the Sixth Army Band at the Presidio military fort in San Francisco, spending time, often while AWOL, in such jazz clubs as the Black Hawk in the Tenderloin and Bop City in the Fillmore district (both clubs really existed), and graduating into a civilian life fraught with glamor and ugliness and every kind of love—thwarted love, and crazy love, and victorious love—above all, the love between these two friends.

Darcy was on the University's insurance plan, and after a journey through a delicate labyrinth of abysses, of blind corners and dead ends, switcheroos and doublecrosses, but with Mrs. Exroy to guide me step by step through the dark, we'd landed Darcy Miller an appointment at the South Austin Medical Associates on Friday, a week following my visit with him. In the meantime, Jerry Sizemore made arrangements to come down for a probably lengthy stay. My former melodramatic mood, the morbid fear and the helpless pity, had given way to a strange giddiness. The truth is that I wondered if out of all this might come three friends— I might be added—I know it's stupid—am I the only grown man who still longs to be friends with other boys?

In the book the two friends Gabriel and Danny refer to each other as "Gee" and "Dee." I noticed that Jerry and Darcy had the same habit—this over the telephone during the course of that week, one conversation with Darcy, and several with Jerry, who called me nightly delivering the good news that again today Darcy had been reachable and happy to chat as he looked forward to meeting his new physician.

The morning of the doctor's appointment I called Darcy three times and got no answer. Each time I left a brief reminder of the appointment along with the assurance I'd be turning up there by 10 a.m. Each time the beep got longer, and each time, as I hung up, the thud in my belly felt a tiny bit more dreadful.

Taking the ranch roads a little too fast I kicked up a

storm of dust that pursued me across the plains and over-ran me when I stopped to unlock and relock each of the gates. I saw no buzzards floating above the Campesino Place, only random cumulus formations that made the morning sky look like a large, comfortable bed. As I eased my vehicle over the creek, I noted that Darcy's Chrysler seemed to have settled more exactly into its place a bit too far from the house, its burgundy hood and convertible top drifted with white seed-fluff from the female cottonwoods.

I knocked on the door while working the knob. It wasn't locked, so I opened it, and although I believed I'd heard a faint shout from somewhere inside, I entered a large, un-filled silence.

"Darcy," I called, "Darcy—are you here?"

"Yeah!" came from the rear of the house.

I followed the sound down the hall past the kitchen and toward the bedroom at the back, which was the master, more or less—the only genuine bedroom—and just inside this bedroom's door lay Darcy Miller on the wooden floor, flat on his back with his head in the hallway, staring out of his watery blue eyes in what I read, upside-down, as bitter-ness. A mess of dried blood covered the floor around his head like a corona, but he didn't seem to be bleeding now. I knelt beside him and could think only of swear words to say, so I said them, and Darcy said, "You got that right."

After a quick run-through of everything I possessed in

the way of remedies and responses, after checking for a pulse and finding none—although Darcy's chest rose and fell and I could hear the breath in his throat—after establishing that he could tell me the date and his name and asking him to take each of my hands and give a squeeze, which he managed all right with equal strength in the right and the left, I abandoned him and called 911 from the phone in the living room. While the emergency dispatcher and I very carefully went over the digits of each gate combination, I noticed that the living room lamp, the overhead light, the one in the hallway—all the lights in the house— were burning, just as I'd left them seven days previous.

With a reluctance I identify, now, as shameful, I returned to Darcy where he lay on the floor still conscious and still peering straight upward. He wore gray sweatpants and one slipper, the other foot bare, and he wore no shirt, though he'd pulled his lab coat and covers from the bed down onto himself and got some protection from those. I recalled an exchange from *The Reason I'm Lost* between Gabe Smith and Danny Osgood—and here, stretched out on the floor with his eyes moving back and forth, poring over the ceiling as if it were a problem in math, was the real, the original, Danny Osgood—this exchange:

Gabe: "How old is that old guy?"

Danny: "Something short of dead."

I went from kitchen to hallway with bath towels and

dish towels and a quart pan spilling tap water, cursing out loud, I'm sure, the whole time, and bringing no real comfort to the old guy on the floor. My heart ached, I tell you, and it's likely I shed some tears, but within half an hour I felt convinced Darcy wouldn't die, and I was going back and forth from the living room window to the hallway, reporting to him on the somewhat comical progress of an ambulance careering toward us over the prairie with its red-white-and-blue lights revolving and the *we-you, we-you* of its siren rising and vanishing in the empty morning and finally cut short with a yip as the van lurched over the creek (not quite sideswiping my Subaru) and a generation of medically trained people hatched out of it and cartwheeled into the house—only four such people, it turned out, but with their equipment, and the scene they created, the ministrations and communications, the gurney and the portable defibrillator and ventilation pump and the blood pressure devices, the fixing of electrodes and the clearing of airways and the search for a useable vein, all accompanied by syncopated cries and whispers, the loud voice of the man on the walkie-talkie and the lower tones of the man and woman establishing intravenous hydration and fitting the oxygen mask, which descended like a judgment to cover Darcy's liverish mouth, and the silent fretting of the fourth technician, a petite baldheaded man, who did nothing, I have to say, but move from one to the other of his cohort, looking over shoulders—they multiplied and magnified themselves. Meanwhile, I used Darcy's phone to call Jerry Sizemore, and by the time I'd filled him in, the ambulance had fled across the creek again toward the ranch road, spinning water from its tires, leaving me alone in the kind of silence following a slap in the face.

I reached the hospital within forty-five minutes—a time nearly doubled while I searched for a parking space—and the ER's doors parted before me with a groan and a sigh and then a thump, and I entered the waiting area. At this moment I had no thought for anyone but Darcy—I was concerned that we were separated, and that without an advocate he'd end up sidelined in a hallway or even a storeroom or a loading dock; I wanted to find Darcy and had no time for comparing this experience with any other—but now, in my pajamas, with the coffee, looking back, I see that the Parkland Community Hospital's emergency room doors opened onto a new phase of my own life, one I can expect to continue until all expectations cease, the phase in which these visits to emergency rooms and clinics increased in frequency and by now have become commonplace: trips with my mother, my father, later my friend Joe, then of course with my friend Link—and eventually me too—the tests, forms, interviews, exams, the journeys into the machines. By the time I reached the hospital, Darcy had been taken well in hand and begun going through all of these things, and probably more. I'd expected to wait in the anteroom among the sick and wounded and their loved ones bent over mystifying paperwork or staring down at their hands, beaten at last not by life but by the refusal of their dramas to end in anything but this meaningless procedural quicksand . . . No, between his visits to the technicians, the staff let me wait with Darcy in the realm behind the veil, in the Trauma Theater, a vast area cut up by moveable white partitions screening my view of the surrounding moaners and weepers and their powerless comforters. Whom I obviously heard.

From time to time as the morning turned to afternoon they wheeled Darcy away on his gurney, leaving me to sit in a three-walled cell in a collapsible chair that was now its only piece of furniture, among all the equipment from which Darcy had been disconnected before his disappearance into the rest of his adventure.

After he was taken away several times and brought back each time, they left us together for a long interval. The 3-to-11-p.m. shift came on and the sun crossed the parking lot and it got half dark outside. Darcy wanted something cold on his tongue. I fed him some pink ice cream from a cup because he didn't seem able to control his fingers. Nobody came. On the back of Darcy's head a patch of scalp had been shaved bald and a square inch of white bandage planted in the middle of it. Every so often—every three or four minutes—he pointed at his head and said, "They gave me a couple stitches." He made errant remarks—they weren't remarks about anything around here. "Nice day with the rain in your face," is one I remember verbatim.

A nurse turned up around 7 p.m., an older woman who carried an air of competence, authority, and goodwill. Darcy's focus seemed unblunted as she began describing the tests he'd been given, and he cut her short—"What's wrong with me?"

"We're going to have to admit you. You'll talk to the oncologist on Monday, but right now—maybe you'd like your friend to leave while we go over the results in privacy."

"He can stay."

"We have some serious information to go over here, is why I suggest—"

"Then go over it, okay? My friend can stay. What's going on here? What is happening to me?"

"The cancer in your lungs has spread, and we're seeing tumors in your brain. A whole lot of tumors, Mr. Miller."

"Cancer in my lungs? What cancer?"

"Were you not aware you have Stage Four lung cancer?"

"I guess I am now. And brain tumors—is that cancer too?"

"Yes. The lung cancer has metastasized. The condition is very advanced."

"So this is the end."

"This is metastatic cancer, Mr. Miller, yes."

"How long? And please don't shit me."

"You can ask the doctor about that. Monday, the oncologist—"

"Nurses know more than doctors."

She looked at me, and then again at Darcy, and then paid us both, I believe, a great compliment by her candor: "A month. A few weeks at the most. But probably not even a month."

Silence while she held Darcy's hand. After a few minutes she left us without a word.

Darcy went on staring upward. I must say, he had the kind of stoic poise I've always felt, personally, would lie far beyond my own reach in such straits. I had no idea what thoughts might be tumbling among the tumors in his head until he frowned at me and said, "Well, hell . . . I might've known. It was Andy Hedges all along, the whole time, from the start to the finish. Andy Hedges."

"Who's Andy Hedges?"

His chest ballooned, and he heaved a sigh. Then—"What?"

"Who's Andy Hedges?"

"I don't know."

Long after night had fallen, Darcy was wheeled on his gurney into an elevator to be taken to a private room. As he traveled, he was sleeping. I tagged along as far as the doors to the elevator. He was still unconscious as I wished him well. The doors closed, and I didn't see him again ever. He became the charge of Jerry Sizemore, who arrived in Austin late the following afternoon. I left Austin on a plane that morning, and Jerry and I didn't quite overlap. These long years later, I still haven't met Jerry Sizemore in the flesh.

Darcy died on the twelfth of June, exactly one month from the time he was admitted to the Parkland Community Hospital and the nurse with the kind face and sincere touch held his hand and predicted that very outcome. Jerry Sizemore, I guess, would have been the one to see to Darcy's affairs and effects, which in the course of Darcy's travels had bled away to nothing. Here in Northern California fifteen years later, in this house where Link has died and where I've stayed on—not only out of exhaustion but also because I've grown stuck in my role, it's become my religion to carry things to and fro in the temple, and I find no reason to adjust right away to the demise of our god—here in this house not haunted, but saturated through-and-through with the life of its dead owner, it falls to me to sort through Link's aggregations of rocks, bricks, broken seashells, tools, books, medicines and medical supplies, firewood, driftwood, lumber, cartons of Quaker Oatmeal, cases of Ensure meal-supplement drink, frozen foods dating back, at least in one of his freezers, eighteen years to 1997, smashed appliances, exploded vehicles, incomplete, irrelevant, or in-

comprehensible documents, and "parts"—that is, agglom-
erated nuts, bolts, shafts, gears, belts, bearings, all on their
way from rust to dust—and small, delicate, though casually
handled boxes holding the memorabilia we call "odds and
ends" because their attachment to any human personality
has been annihilated: an old tintype portrait of a darkly
wooden face neither male nor female, an acorn encased in
a cube of clear Plexiglas, medallions and badges in plastic
envelopes, other such things—a snow globe, its surface so
worn you can't see what it holds, but by its heft you know
the water still submerses the wintry scene inside, while nobody who ever beheld it remains alive.

I came across a scarf among Link's things, a gift he'd
intended for Elizabeth, his former wife, a yellow silk scarf
folded up in soft white paper and laid in a small red box
with a card bearing two words—

For Liz

Liz was the only woman Link had truly loved, he con-
fided in me many times, as his body and mind failed him in
his deranged bedroom with the dangerous wood-burning
stove surrounded by the tottering stacks of flammable publications . . . I often observed him lying in bed, holding his
cellphone in one hand and in the other a can of charcoal-
lighting fluid—his little trick was to stretch his long left leg

out and hook the stove's door handle by his toe, flick it open with a simian flair, and train an incendiary stream into the flames within to produce a small-scale explosion followed by five minutes of hard, bright burning (poor circulation gave him cold extremities), meanwhile yacking on the phone with Liz, who lived in San Mateo a hundred miles away. She and Link had been married and parted decades before.

The daughter of Japanese immigrants, Liz, a black-haired beauty even now in her sixties, had become in recent years a physically quite tentative and cautious person, with a ceremonious, exploratory footstep, because she no longer had any idea where she was going or where she'd been as recently as two seconds ago, her memory and identity wiped away by Alzheimer's disease. But she stayed serene and cheerful, and greeted everyone, whether a lifelong acquaintance or a brand-new face, with a hug and a smile, saying, "Hello, stranger."

Of the scores of family and friends who adored and supported Liz—in fact, of all the human beings in the world—Link was the only person she recognized. And in this world, which is only Now, she knows him perfectly, as if they've just risen from their custom-made king-plus-size waterbed—have I mentioned he was six foot nine, a sliver over two meters tall?—the two of them beautiful and young, and rich from his many business enterprises. Liz doesn't know her husband Malcolm, a retired U.S. naval captain who sees to her every need and even calls Link's telephone number for her nightly; and nightly Liz and Link talk on the phone and she pledges her love, and Link, who has never for a minute considered, in his own heart and mind, the marriage ended, drinks in these declarations and answers them with his own in the midst of a world without forward or backward, without logic, like the world of dreams, thanks to Liz's dementia and to Link's opiated vagueness and diabetic spikes in blood sugar, his occasional insulin psychosis, and the cycles of delirium driven by the ebb and flow of toxins, mainly ammonia, in his bloodstream.

Liz rarely left her own home in San Mateo, but Malcolm was willing to bring her north for a visit. She knew Link's voice, and we hoped she would recognize Link's face too, though they hadn't been physically present to one another for many years. Link vowed to me he would live to see Liz again. Liz, of course, had no idea any of this was being considered. Because taking her places was a matter requiring a lot of care and strategy—and time—Link was forced to count the days and hang on.

For more than a week at the start of April, while he lay finally unable to leave his bed, stretched out to his full six feet nine inches diagonally across his mattress with his orange tomcat Friedrich asleep on his chest, a succession of storms, three of them, all of tropical origin, had swept in from the ocean to do violence, and now a fourth disturbance, not the worst of the crop, but impressive enough, had the crowns of the hundred-foot redwoods churning in the gulley behind the house. At least a couple of times each day the house lost electric power, and in the chair by the stove I would have to stop reading my book and listen to Link and his cat snoring between thunderclaps.

In the middle of one of these outages, about three in the afternoon, Link called me to his bedside and demanded to be brought to his room. I told him that's where we were—in his room.

"It looks like my room," he said, "but this is not my room."

Link . . . except for the eyes peering out of his hairless skull he looked no different than a corpse, but his thoughts were alive. And he wasn't always appropriately oriented. You had to be careful with him.

"What does your room look like?"

"It looks a lot like this one, but this room isn't the right room. Do you understand? This is not my room."

"So—you want to go to your room."

He saw I didn't get it. As if translating each phrase for me into my hopeless foreigner's tongue, he then said: "I wish . . . to proceed . . . to the chamber . . . which is mine."

"First of all," I said, "I don't know where you want to go. Second of all, there's nobody here but me. How am I going to get you on your feet all by myself?"

As if gravity had been revoked, he rose to his full height and took three strides to the sliding doors of his bedroom.

"Link. Link. Where are you going?"

With a sweep of his arm he pushed aside the glass pane, and the outdoors rolled into the room. He stood for a few seconds with the rain spitting in his face, then stepped into the storm.

Should you ask—it never occurred to me to prevent him. I followed him into the dark afternoon. He stood swaying in the yard, which sloped gently for a hundred feet before plunging into the mile-long gulley that ran down toward the ocean, or rather down toward the roaring extinction into which ocean, earth, and sky had disappeared. For a moment Link took the measure of something, perhaps of this shot of strength he'd received, then like a performer on stilts he set his distant feet walking, steering himself through three kinds of thunder, that of the gusting wind, that of the drunken ocean, and the thunderclaps following the lightning. I described the redwoods as churning, but their motion better resembled a towering shrug—in a storm the redwoods seem to me punished, resigned, while the cypress trees seem out of their minds, throwing their limbs around hysterically. As I trailed Link closely through this flickering chaos, he in a Peruvian herder's cap, pajama bottoms, barefoot, barechested under a long ragged bathrobe open and flapping in the gusts, it seemed to me inescapable that he meant to stumble-march down into the gulley, the sopping brambles and tangles, the thunder, the sea's embrace, and never come back. I was mistaken. He soon banked left, and circled around the corner of the house to balance in front of his bedroom's back door—situated about sixteen feet diagonally across this bedroom from the sliding doors he'd walked out of. The journey had covered thirty or forty paces and lasted under ninety seconds. The weather was more wind than rain—Link was spattered, but not soaked, as he sloughed off his robe, lay down in bed, thanked me for my help in getting him to his proper room, and immediately began dying.

Until the consummate couple of hours, Link was able to hear me and talk to me. I asked him if I should kill him with the morphine, and he said no. He preferred to wrestle with his torment, sitting up in bed, pivoting right and left, putting his feet on the floor, hunching over and rocking, curling into a ball, straightening out on the bed, lying east, lying west, no position bearable for more than a few seconds—more active in this single afternoon than I'd seen him in the last two months put together—and he wanted no help with this. As Link understood it, the doctrine of his spiritual teacher nine thousand miles away in India required him to live each incarnation to the last natural breath, which came for him about nine o'clock that night in a long, gently vocal sigh. But before that, around seven, he spoke to me for the first time in an hour or so—"Is Liz coming?" "I think she was coming about eight," I said. "What are you doing?" he asked me—"sitting shiva?"—his last words. His fight gave out and for the rest of it he lay on his back breathing like a sump pump with lengthy stops and convulsive, snorting resumptions, terrible to listen to, but only at first, and after that a sort of comfort.

An hour into this phase, almost exactly at 8 p.m., Liz arrived. She entered Link's bedroom by the back door, as mindful as a tightrope walker, measuring her steps against the void, assisted by her husband Malcolm. As Malcolm continued through the kitchen to join me in the dining room, Liz went down on her knees at the bedside with her arms stretched out straight across Link's breast, her face pressed into the mattress.

Malcolm sat beside me at the cluttered dining table, some distance from the bedroom but with an angle of view on his wife. Even here on the other side of the house, and despite the dull booming of the weather all around, we could hear Link's respiratory system at work. In the high winds the house seemed similarly unconscious but alive, the walls and windowpanes trembling. Malcolm had gone to generous lengths in order to get Liz here for this last meeting and parting with Link, just as he not only enabled but encouraged their telephone conversations, pressing himself into these services out of some poetic inkling, I'm willing to assume, some unbearable intuition of the rightness and even the beauty of the facts. He had a round, clean face drained long ago of any sadness or happiness. We sat side by side and said nothing, did nothing.

After forty-five minutes, Malcolm left me and entered the bedroom. Liz stood up and said, "Night-night, Linkie. I love you." She turned to embrace her husband of twenty-five years and said, "Hello, stranger," and they went out the door. I heard their car pull away, and ten minutes after that Link was dead. The storm continued till about 3 a.m. while I sat by the stove and while the cat Friedrich, made stark in the flashes of lightning, marched restlessly over the boxes and bags and piles. There was nothing to be done. I didn't want to trouble the hospice staff or the mortuary people until morning, and there was no one else to call. As with Darcy Miller at the end, so with Link—down to a couple of friends.

In the last decade and a half I've corresponded a bit with Jerry Sizemore, but he hasn't volunteered to tell me about Darcy Miller's last days, and I haven't invited him to. I understand, however, that Jerry Sizemore sat at Darcy's bedside every day, all day, for thirty-one days, until Darcy took his final breath.

I got that story from Mrs. Exroy. I encountered her now and again during the next few years, over the course of which I got back to Austin several times to teach as a guest professor, and whenever I ran into Mrs. Exroy, usually while she stood smoking an extra-long filtered cigarette behind the Brewer House, flicking her sparks and ashes into the ravine, Darcy Miller's death was the first topic of our conversation, and she described for me each time, as if for the first time, Jerry's faithful attendance at his friend's bedside those last thirty-one days. Then after four or five years Mrs. Exroy and I stopped bumping into each other, because she died too. Oh—and just a few weeks ago in Marin County my friend Nan, Robert's widow—if you recall my shocking phone call with Nan at the very top of this account—took sick and passed away. It doesn't matter. The world keeps turning. It's plain to you that at the time I write this, I'm not dead. But maybe by the time you read it.

DOPPELGÄNGER,

POLTERGEIST

~~~~~

Yesterday, January 8, 2016, marked the eighty-first anniversary of Elvis Presley's birth. It's now two days since I learned that the poet Marcus Ahearn (we call him Mark) was arrested, or detained, one week ago, for making a ruckus at the Presley family's Graceland Mansion in Memphis. In fact Mark was taken into custody for disturbing, or trying to disturb, the site of Elvis Presley's grave. The shenanigans of a poet don't rate headlines. I learned of Mark's troubles through mutual friends. And I reflect to myself that he's been taken, at last, into the jaws of the powers he's vexed and bedeviled for nearly forty years: I say forty years because I happen to know that on August 29, 1977, while still a juvenile, Mark took part in an attempt by several persons to rob Presley's original grave in the Forest Hill Cemetery in Memphis, which attempt—never alluded to in the press without the adjective "bizarre"—resulted in the transfer of Elvis's remains, along with those of his mother Gladys Love Smith Presley, to the security of the Graceland estate, where mother and son now rest side by side in matching copper coffins weighing nine hundred pounds each . . . And Mark confessed to me, person to person, that shortly after midnight on January 8, 2001, under the feeble light of a crescent moon, he entered the Priceville Cemetery near Tupelo, Mississippi, took a shovel to an unmarked grave, dug down to the miniature coffin interred there, and broke it open intending to despoil it of its contents, namely the infant corpse of Elvis Presley's twin brother, Jesse Garon Presley, born dead.

To the extent we possess a roster of genuine poets, Marcus Ahearn is certainly listed there. I first met him in 1984, when I taught a poetry workshop at Columbia. Mark was in his twenties. I was thirty-five. I'd headed a few such workshops in the previous decade, pored over and struggled with the verses of all sorts of students, not only the grads in the writing workshops but also tiny children in state-funded "poetry-in-the-schools" programs, retirees in community arts center classes, and once, for over a year, robbers, smugglers and thugs in a federal prison, and I'd wondered, more or less constantly: Are my own attempts any better than theirs? Marcus Ahearn's first half-dozen poems delivered my answer. They were the real thing, line after line of the real thing, and as I held them in my hands a secret anguish relaxed its grip on my heart, and I accepted that I'd never be a poet, only a teacher of poets.

Mark got himself up for the role in tweed blazers and baggy corduroys and bulky cardigans. He had a poet's stormy auburn locks. His face was very pleasing: clean-shaven and like a doll's, with round, bright blue doll's eyes and pink doll's cheeks. Button nose, small mouth, a charming smile often displayed. Altogether winning. When he entered the classroom, you could feel the welcome. The others didn't seem to hold his talent against him. Maybe they were blind to it.

Now. Where did my involvement with this thing begin? In that Columbia classroom, it stands to reason, with its gouged wooden floorboards, tall windows, distant ceiling— an excess of acoustical space that created, in my own ears anyway, a reverberation mocking everything we said. I suppose we surrounded a seminar table and these gifted students from all walks of life explored fresh ideas in an atmosphere of intellectual generosity and mutual support while I got bored, then irritated, and finally desperate to hear something stupid and silly. It was time, in other words, to hear from the professor. It's likely I started with an anecdote, one of my favorites, about Frank Sinatra: After singing "America the Beautiful" to the assembled 1956 Democratic National Convention, Sinatra was approached by seventy-four-year-old twenty-two-term Texas Congressman Sam Rayburn, at that time and for the previous sixteen years the Speaker of the House of Representatives, who grasped the crooner's arm and begged, "Sing 'The Yellow Rose of Texas,' son," to which Sinatra replied: "Hands off the suit, creep." That probably brought to mind another of Sinatra's quips, furnished sometime in 1955, when he described the rock-and-roll music of Elvis Presley as "a rancid-smelling

aphrodisiac." Elvis!—And just like that, I'm twisting in the
snares of passion and memory, rehearsing for the young-
sters the night in 1957 when I, a third-grader, sat in a
theater packed mostly with teenagers, and we all clapped
along to Elvis Presley's numbers in *Jailhouse Rock,* the
whole of us making a single sinister, infantile, sexual en-
tity governed only by a jungle rhythm in the dark—"only
by the pulse," I bet I said, "of our very gore." Here would
have been a smart point on which to pivot toward some
aspect of our studies—rhythm, for Christ's sake—but instead I fall prey to compulsive ruminations, I talk at far too
great a length of my bewilderment that the vapid, tedious
Elvis of later years seemed nothing like the Elvis of 1957.
"The uninformed," I probably said, "blame the change on
drug abuse, but I blame Presley's manager, 'Colonel' Tom
Parker, a lethal champion of mediocrity. By 1957 Parker
had already begun injecting his paralytic ooze into the fiery
whirling original fact that was Elvis Presley, and in early
1958, he turned him over to the U.S. military to be rendered down to glue." Here, I'm sure, I'd have tried to snap
my mouth shut with a remark I often deliver: "It wasn't the
Kennedy assassination in 1963 that broke the back of the
American century—it was Elvis Presley's enlistment in the
army in 1958"—directly upon which the world witnessed
the evaporation of Elvis, the shearing of his sideburns, the
photos of him trussed up in a uniform with shiny gold but-

tons, the announcement that the slender, smoldering andro-
gyne of *Jailhouse Rock* had taken up the study of karate.
And this transformation was instigated by "Colonel" Tom
Parker, "who was no kind of colonel, but only an infantry
private, cashiered from the U.S. Army as both a deserter
and a psychopath." Am I pounding on the table? Somebody
is. "And listen to me! Heed me now! Inside every one of
us lives a poisoner like Colonel Tom Parker." By this time
I've risen to my feet, I'm shouting, probably weeping—my
marriage, I forgot to say, is confused; my finances are on
fire; and my tenure-track job as a teacher of poetry at this
prestigious university hangs by a thread, a circumstance
having nothing to do with my teaching, which is inept, or
my poems, which are fraudulent, and everything to do with
departmental politics, at which I fail—so, yes, shouting and
weeping, I instruct my students to leave me now, get out,
go home—"go sit before your desk without a pen, without
paper, without words even. Reach into your heart and pull
out your own Colonel Parker from inside you, open your
jaws, gnash him down, let him be pulped in your guts and
ejected as shit—that's right, erupt!—and bring *that* to me
smeared on a page!" And from the first word to the last of
this monolog the young and talented Marcus Ahearn would
have been staring at my face, his doll's eyes shining, although at that moment, exercised as I was, I couldn't have
noticed.

In all likelihood this was the day I slammed the class-room's door behind me, sailed down the hall to the office of the Director of Columbia University's Program in Creative Writing, a nice, nice man, and said to him, "Fuck you. And your program. And these students. It's a crime to encourage them. I quit." And so on, and quite a bit more. This man dealt with me adroitly. He kept his hands folded before him on the desk, fingers laced together, his head cocked, and listened. At five-second intervals, he nodded. He neither supported nor contradicted me when I said that Ahearn was a poet and the others were congenital mediocrities, that our writing program amounted to an academic Ponzi scheme, a literary racket . . . After I ran out of words he cleared his throat, assured me he could appreciate the torsion and doubt I labored under, praised my candor, my valor, even, and got me to promise I wouldn't leave these young people in the lurch but would finish out the semester, which consisted, after all, of only three more class meetings. He shook my hand. We parted friends. His name was Dusseldorf. He'd written some books and nobody had bought them, and now—he did this. I went down the hall-ways and stairways and out into the April twilight of Manhattan's upper west side and walked the streets and waited for sundown to close the lid on one of my life's top five most embarrassing episodes.

The lid, however, wouldn't shut. The mind held back the whole sky. The mind rehearsed the recent scene, explained, denied, composed, revised, all in a whining voice. Meanwhile, the city shrieked and throbbed. Manhattan in the 1980s had a pulse, heady, potent, but like a wound's. Do you remember? Death-camp homeless. Guerrilla vendors. Three-card monte. Trash all over the streets. How I survived this attack on multiple fronts, how I crossed those streets without getting murdered by a vehicle, I can't imagine. Maybe Marcus Ahearn saved me. This might have been the day Mark Ahearn strolled up beside me in the middle of the crosswalk and took my arm and said "Professor Harrington!—another dismal classroom performance," and our friendship began.

It might easily have been that day. I'm only guessing. So what? The Past just left. Its remnants, I claim, are mostly fiction. We're stranded here with the threadbare patchwork of memory, you with yours, I with mine, and in mine I'm sitting with Marcus Ahearn twenty minutes later in a park plaza I often retreated to in those days, a tiny green triangle where 106th crosses Broadway and then, immediately, West End Avenue: a couple of benches among budding oaks, random pigeons, eager squirrels, and big river rats, too, migrants from the Hudson just blocks away, assimilated by the upper west side culture and now living as squirrels.

These rats stand upright, beg, feed from the human hand. Mark and I sip coffee from go-cups, and, "You're very passionate," he said, "about Elvis Presley."

"All of that just leapt out."

"Leapt out," he agreed, "and ran around with no pants."

"A point was being made."

"About Colonel Tom Parker."

"The colonel ruined Elvis. The colonel leached him and bleached him."

Mark pried the lid from his go-cup and peered down at the dregs and interrogated them: "Does Columbia University care, even slightly, what goes on in the classroom? I mean"—now he looked at me—"your fits and your breakdowns."

"Conniptions."

"Do they trouble you about your outbursts?"

Yes, I was crazy. Somewhere between the covers of a heavy textbook, my diagnosis waited for me. But at this moment I was Professor Kevin Peter Harrington conferring with a student, duty-bound to guard him from the abyss that constitutes my inner world, the abyss "that separates us," as the poet Nicanor Parra remarked, "from the other abysses."

So I just said, "You write wonderfully."

"It's not the most important thing I do."

Then he shut up. I felt prompted to ask the obvious

question—I felt prodded, and so I dug in my heels and didn't ask him what was the most important thing.

He changed the subject without breaking stride. "You're right to call the colonel lethal."

"Who called him lethal?"

"'A lethal champion of mediocrity'—you called him that."

"Good for me."

"The colonel, you know, was suspected of murdering a woman in his youth. Lethal. It ties right in with a theory I have about Elvis's life and death."

"Why this fascination with Elvis Presley? Aren't you way out of date? How old are you?"

"Last September I turned twenty-four." And he gave me the particulars: Charles Marcus Ahearn (but he didn't mention the Charles; the Charles came out later), born September 10, 1959, in the Washington suburb of Potomac, Maryland; father a physician, a specialist in liver ailments, and for nearly twenty years the assistant director of the National Institutes of Health; mother a Smith College valedictorian, respected amateur bibliographer (of the poets Marianne Moore and Elizabeth Bishop), and activist in the cause of animal rights. Mark attended public schools, graduating in 1977 from Potomac's Winston Churchill High, the only such institution I know of named for someone not an American. Mark's parents, old enough to be his grandparents, raised him in an atmosphere of kindly tolerance and good order, and, at the time of our conversation in the plaza, mother and father still lived together in the house Mark had known from infancy to age eighteen, when he'd left them to attend Williams College. The sudden death of his only sibling, a brother eleven years older than Mark, delivered his childhood's single abiding injury. Employed for the summer in a national forest somewhere in the Northwest ahead of his freshman debut at Harvard, this brother, Lancaster, nicknamed Lance, had plunged from the upper boughs of a very tall evergreen. What he was doing up there, I couldn't ask. What if it was something silly, a drunken bet, a youngster's manic, simian impulse or seizure? Or worse—suicide?

"My brother Lance," Mark said, "was a legendary youth. He had this negligent charisma, completely irresistible to other kids his age, and younger ones too, like me, all of us floundering in a pimply mess while Lance lived out every minute as if he'd rehearsed for it, this cool rocker with jeans and boots and an old MG roadster that used to be red and had no top—but he flew all around Montgomery County in it, winter and summer, rain and snow, sort of blazing a trail in the sky. The girls worshipped him; he had his pick of them; he must have deflowered dozens. In a fight, he was like Errol Flynn, dancing around as if his opponents were hired to make him look invincible. He laughed at authority—got himself suspended from school several times each year, and he didn't care. And neither did Mom and Dad. When Lance was around, they were speechless. They were like a woodcutter and the woodcutter's wife in their thatched hut in a European folk tale: They understood they'd reared some kind of magical giant. The quests, and the voyages, and the kingdoms he'd win—it was so much fun imagining Lance's future. Hang the infractions—the school principal helped him talk his way into Harvard. Then he was dead."

"I'm sorry."

"Cards on the table. Did you know about my juvenile criminal record?"

"No."

"My youthful indiscretions?"

"Mark, you're still in your youth."

"The thing with Elvis's grave?"

"What are you talking about? I don't know what you're talking about."

"Seven years ago, I spent four days in the juvenile lockup in Memphis for trying to dig up his grave."

"Whose grave?"

"Elvis Presley's, man. Elvis."

"What?"

"I'll give you the short version: The day after Elvis died I took a Greyhound bus to Memphis and walked thirty-one blocks to the Graceland Mansion. I was one of the thousands of mourners standing outside in the rain. I was sixteen. I met a pack of fools who said they were going to dig up Elvis's grave, which was across town at the Forest Hill Cemetery, in a hole three days old. I went along, and we all got pinched.

"It turned out the whole thing was sort of a ruse, a publicity stunt. Nobody could have got into that vault. They didn't even bring a shovel. Later came rumors that the vandals had been hired by the Presley family. They just wanted to show how vulnerable the site was, so the grave could be moved to the Graceland Mansion. At Graceland, the family get fifteen million bucks a year from tourists.

"I wasn't charged with anything. I stayed in a sort of dorm for runaways. After a few days the prosecutor declined to pursue the case, and I went home on a plane.

"All of this happened because I was out of my mind over Elvis Presley's death. I'm going to explain. My brother Lance was obsessed with Elvis Presley and collected all his records . . . No. Let me start again:

"I have another brother—also dead.

"Have you ever heard the term 'twinless twin'? My brother was one of those, a twinless twin, with an identical twin brother born dead beside him.

"Elvis Presley was the same—his twin brother Jesse was stillborn.

"Maybe because of that historical coincidence, my brother was nuts on the subject of Elvis, touched, obsessed. Lance owned—conscientiously collected—every one of Elvis's recordings up to the moment of his death—Lance's death, I mean—and I inherited that collection and added to it and kept it complete up to the moment of his death— Elvis's death. Three hundred and eighty-six vinyl discs, eventually—every album, every single, even the corny Christmas and gospel stuff, all the way back to 'It's All Right Mama.' Lance bequeathed half of it to me, and I kept collecting. As of two days before Elvis's death, I had everything, and all the covers—the covers are what the collectors want, even more than the records themselves—I had everything.

"But here's a terrible fact: As of the day Elvis died—I didn't have any of it, not any more.

"Less than twenty-four hours before Elvis was found dead on his bathroom floor, I had boxed up and shipped off my dead brother's collection of every one of his recordings. Like a faithful priest, I had kept up the collection until what none of us knew would be the very last one—'Way On Down,' which peaked at thirty-one on the *Billboard* charts—I thought, 'This man has become pitiful, and my brother's dead, and I need money for college'—that's how I phrased it, though of course my folks paid my way entirely, and I just wanted a little jingle in my pockets. I didn't even need that. I had a few hundred. I'd just spent the summer working as a landscaper's grunt, the most horrible summer of my life, and I didn't want any kind of job, not even a part-time cafeteria job . . . Eleven boxes weighing forty-nine pounds. Took it to the PO, sent it certified and insured for four thousand U.S. dollars, the purchase price. The cashier's check was already on the way to me from Alberta, Canada.

"The next morning I turned on the news and learned of the death, the previous night, of Elvis Presley. It skewered my heart, Kev—can I call you Kev?"

"Nobody calls me Kev."

"I want to."

"Go ahead, then."

"—and my mind snapped, my soul sickened, and I went to Memphis. It was either that, or kill the dog."

I've condensed the tale, and the time it took to tell this much of it. Twilight had filled the streets. A cold draft rolled in from the Hudson along 106th, stinking like the river. The pigeons and squirrels had retired for the night, and the rats too. A homeless man slept under newspapers and blankets on the only other bench, and a second man sat on the ground nearby with his back against a tree and his worldly belongings bundled beside him and his blanket wrapped around his shoulders, giving us the evil eye. It was clear we occupied his bed. But Mark had taken me by the nose. I was his prompter—and more, confessor—as he led me toward that part of the world labeled on the old charts "Here Be Monsters."

"What dog?"

"My brother's little bulldog—Sinbad. My folks took him in."

"Why on earth would you kill—"

"It's just an expression, Kev. —Hey, you know, my brother Lance described almost the same experience you did with the *Jailhouse Rock* film. He was in the third grade too. If your bio in the back of the *Young Poets* anthology is correct, you're thirty-five, right? You guys would be almost exactly the same age."

"Should I feel a little bit uncomfortable that you're talking like that? Sort of roping me into a family scenario?"

"Sure, go ahead and feel uncomfortable. Feel free." I laughed, and Mark said, "My brother had a theory about Elvis Presley and the murderous colonel—nobody buys this theory, but to me it makes a lot of sense. I think it can be proven. Proving it is my life's work."

"The most important thing you do."

"Right."

"More important than your talent and your art."

"Correct."

"Exploring a theory about a marquee idol. And how will this theory be proven?"

"Through the amassing of facts."

"And are you going to tell me what this theory is?"

"Next time."

We'd stood up to exchange our parting gestures. The bench's owner had arranged himself on the bench with his cup presented for alms. I went over to make a contribution and instead created a scene. The poor guy swore at me viciously, obscenely, with savage skill: I had just plunked two germy quarters into his fresh cup of coffee. Now what? Back then you really didn't know—at any moment Manhattan could shank you, finish you off. Mark Ahearn appeared at my side and bailed me out with a five-dollar bill. We said good night.

~~~~~

Mark and I took an early dinner together after each of the semester's three remaining classes, and then we didn't meet again in person until 1990. During this period of half a dozen years, the early years of my acquaintance with Mark, parallel to our friendly correspondence but quite independent of it, I found Marcus Ahearn's verse becoming essential to me. I called him on the phone two or three times a year to get an update on his publications, to hear his kind voice, and to ask for poems. He was good enough to send me a few now and then, once the manuscript for an upcoming book. Also Mark sent me cassette tapes of himself singing songs of his own devising, unaccompanied, in a voice a lot like Elvis's voice, with an echo, as if he'd recorded them—where? In a trash can? He published his first two books, won a couple of awards, remained single, and relocated frequently, filling lucrative visiting-professor posts of the kind available to top-tier literary figures nowadays at university writing programs who get the good ones in, wring a few words of wisdom out of them, and send them along before they start angling for something tenure-track. That was Mark, the itinerant professor, and it still is. As for Marcus Ahearn, the poet—much the same. He'd distinguished himself by traveling his own orbit, and his aesthetic territory didn't crowd anyone else's. Among readers of poetry, rarefied and meager as that audience may be, he'd become part of the stellar map. His writing was important.

But it wasn't the most important thing he did.

Mark's brother Lance, a twinless twin, had bequeathed him all the vinyl records of Elvis Presley, another twinless twin. Negligent of the deep personal authority of these gifts, Mark let them slip from his grasp—worse: sold them for money. In the ensuing guilty years, Mark's obsession with Elvis flourished even more wildly than his brother's and came to focus on one particular thread of his brother's interest in the rock 'n' roll King—the brother's theory, or hypothesis, that the Elvis Presley found dead on his bathroom floor the afternoon of August 16, 1977, the Elvis Presley who had lived in the Graceland Mansion for nearly twenty years, was not Elvis Presley; that in the spring of 1957 Colonel Tom Parker arranged for the disappearance—the assassination, the willful murder—of the King and his replacement by a quisling Elvis, that is, by his lost twin brother Jesse Garon Presley, falsely believed to have been stillborn, "but living all along in Memphis," Ahearn told me, "with his adopted mother, Sarah Jane Restell, the demon midwife who stole him the night of his birth."

"I don't have legal-standard proof of every detail, no, but hang on to your hat," he told me on the telephone one morning in a conversation that got unnecessarily distended by his enthusiasm, unnecessarily, I say, because he'd called me, in the first place, to tell me he was staying at a cabin only a few miles from my house, and to invite me over for breakfast—but he couldn't pause his monolog ten minutes to let me drive over and lend him an actual ear—"because as of yesterday's mail delivery, Kev, I've got dead solid proof that the brother and his adopted mother existed. I've got the documents right here on this kitchen table," he said on the phone, and now I was hurrying through the messy, off-and-on Cape Cod winter like somebody out of Hitchcock: I would arrive to find him stretched out with his throat cut, and all the documents, the dead solid proof, vanished.

I was living, then, in Wellfleet, where my wife Anne Hayes had inherited a rambling old wooden house built in

1795. Mark was house-sitting on Slocum Pond, a lonely neighborhood during the off-season, in a cabin that had probably been the original pondside dwelling, early 1800s construction, very low ceilings, drafty and creaky, like Anne's and mine, only smaller, and, thanks to surrounding leafless oaks, even sadder than ours. But Ahearn had sweetened the atmosphere of his house with brewing coffee.

After six years, he looked the same. I think he wore the same tweed jacket. In the claustrophobic kitchen he put his hands on my shoulders and gazed at me at arm's length, and said, "Where are my words?" I took that for a welcome. Mark was excited by his newly acquired documents, but first we had to walk the dog. While the evidence lay in open view on the kitchen table, Mark and I turned up our collars and tagged along with Sinbad the Second, a wizened pit bull who inquired with a scientific deliberateness all around the pond, stopping often to shiver but not to do his business. Contravening local ordinances, he traveled unleashed. "I'll never put a leash on him," Mark said. He lived here with this one companion, reading and writing. After a noticeable silence, he'd recently published a book of technically baffling poems, with line breaks so arbitrary and frequent as to be useless, arrhythmic. On the page they look like some of Charles Bukowski's skinny, chatty, muttering-stuttering antiverses. Impossibly, Mark's words make music, the faraway strains of an irresistible jazz. It's plain to any reader, within a few lines—well, go read the poems and see. Marcus Ahearn trafficks with the ineffable. He makes the mind of the speaker present, in that here-and-now where the reader actually reads—that place. Such a rare thing. Samuel Beckett. Jean Follain, Ionesco—the composer Billy Strayhorn. Mark called his process "psychic improvisation" and referred me to the painter Paul Klee; the term was Klee's. "You just get out a pen and a notebook and let your mind go long," he told me. I could see he needed to talk. He spoke of the power of the spiral currents of water, winds, and metaphysical energies that had sculpted the Cape's curlicue tail, about ten miles from the tip of which we were situated at the moment, here at Slocum Pond among the green pines and malformed black oaks, adding—did Ahearn—that he'd revised his thinking as to reincarnation and now believed the concept to be solely metaphorical, "just another word game, even if the saints and Buddhas are playing it," and who was I to argue about things like reincarnation? My own treatment of the matter went no farther than to pray it was a fiction, this single current addled existence of mine being vastly more than enough. For months I'd been getting the runaround about a new contract from my publisher, and I'd recently flubbed an interview at the University of Michigan, and my wife of seven years was driving, at that second, up Route 6 to an 11 a.m. appointment in Hyannis with a divorce attorney. From horizon to horizon the sky was stuffed with dark clouds—not just a metaphor, but also the scene over our actual heads, a mute, shrunken Cape Cod winter. "Well," I said, "if the saints think reincarnation's a game worth playing . . ." Mark said: "I mean, sure, something's happening over and over, but what? Maybe it's just the breath in and out of our lungs." I pointed out we didn't need a metaphor for breathing—"You just talked about it quite literally." Mark laughed and draped his arm around my shoulders and asked me if I'd heard of a book called *Timeshare with the King*, and I said of course not, and the same for its authors, Ron and Opal Bright.

I've looked at it since: In April 1958, two weeks following Elvis's entry into the U.S. Army, an Arkansas farmer in his fresh-seeded field of sorghum watches a figure coming toward him over the rows—"stopped about ten yards distant, stood looking out toward the horizon—a lad in blue jeans, white teeshirt, motorcycle boots—then turns his gazing eyes on me, Ron Blaine Bright, who said instantly—You are the King!"

Elvis the apparition said: "Ron, Your Aunt Grace in Kimbro, Texas, has gone on. She was strolling the gold streets of Paradise with me this morning. She sent me here to tell you." Then turned and walked back across the fields—"and left real and solid boot-prints through the loam, till the path"—and out of sight.

Arriving home, the farmer Bright found a telegram stuck in the screen door: Yes, Aunt Grace—gone on.

The whole thing, remarkable as it was, went out of mind when his wife Opal came in from the orchard behind the house and said, "Ron, I just watched Elvis Presley walking around in the pear trees. And he talked to me just as usual as anything." Ron said, "I saw him too!"—"Did he tell you your Aunt Grace went to her reward?" Opal asked, and Ron showed her the yellow paper from Western Union.

"The thing is," Ron Blaine Bright points out, "if Elvis was with Aunt Grace in Paradise and all, doesn't that mean he'd gone on too? But how could Elvis be dead, if he was over there in Fort Hood with the U.S. Army?" A question neither he nor Opal confronted at the time.

Later, at supper, Opal said, "Don't look at me!" She put her napkin over her pretty face and said, "There's something I didn't want to say before. The King told me he'd take me to Paradise."

The very next evening, Ron Bright recalls, the poltergeist began its nightly visits, "moaning a little the way only the King could moan, rattling and clanking, especially in the kitchen, no real rough stuff, and no breakage." A principal trick was to turn on the kitchen radio loudly and abruptly when an Elvis song was playing. Another was to fiddle with the family's bottle of honey, which they often found in the mornings overturned and spilling its sweet contents on the pantry floor.

The book, divided into neat halves, continues with the account of Opal Bright, who depicts herself as also dripping honey, "a twenty-year-old woman forty miles from town," sozzling in her nightshift on the porch swing with her knee hiked, and she reveals almost immediately, in paragraph one, that her liaison with the King "began with his call like a touch," improved to distant glimpses from the bedroom window, then became a tickling, sickly, hopeless "thing that took a good, hard hold." She depicts herself as burning and barefoot, wandering through a southern night suffocatingly aromatic with new blossoms, many of them vaguely visible as she passed, their daylight colors washed by the moon and stars to a uniform eggplant, or aubergine. In the cool mown grass, or on the wide cowhide seat of a Model D John Deere tractor, or in other "tender and intimate places," Opal Bright and the King formed their bond, and pretty soon, thanks to Ron Bright's generous spirit, "me and the King, and Ron," his wife reports, "had a timeshare going in the bedroom.

"The King said he'd take me to Paradise. He didn't lie."

The timeshare in Paradise lasted over a year, until the house burned down and the Brights sold for nothing and pulled out for Indianapolis.

The pamphlet concludes with a two-page interview of the Brights together, "Interviewer" not named, describing how they managed. Opal knew: "Ron, it's time for a visit." She felt the touch. Elvis was always considerate, pleasant, "soft with his hands and voice," agreed the husband and wife, and the King was both "respectful and regretful," Ron Bright said, "about having to ask me to leave the bedroom for their time alone. But I never minded it"—nor minded that during the interview his wife called Elvis "the lover of my lifetime." The wife and husband both agreed that above all, Elvis was sad, "ghostly and sad."

~~~~~~~

Like a cat, Sinbad II leapt onto a kitchen chair and started napping. Mark poured coffee into two cups resting between burners on the gas range—the kitchen table being occupied by his display of documentary loot. "Altogether, the bits of evidence on this table cost me just over three grand." He plucked up a page by its corner—"Estes, Franks and Herman. Big Memphis law firm. Greedy about their fees, but I can trust their investigators." Tapping the paper: "Estes hangs out with John Grisham."

He began to read: " 'Anthony Rogers Restell, born January eight, nineteen thirty-five, mother Sarah Jane Restell, father unknown, birth certificate copy attached. Graduated

Central High School, 1953. No Social Security number on record.'

" 'In answer to your queries,' blah blah . . . the difference between computerized files and filed documents, boring, boring . . . Here we go: 'We can state with certainty that Anthony Rogers Restell has generated no record of activity in the U.S. since 1975. With less certainty, but with confidence, we can state that since graduating from Central High School in Memphis in June 1953, Anthony Rogers Restell has left no state or federal record of activity in the U.S. Conclusion: The Anthony Rogers Restell named on the attached birth certificate is (1) deceased without record, or (2) permanently relocated overseas, or (3) living in the U.S. under a long-established alias.'

"Last, but not least—'Please advise if you would like copies of Central High School yearbooks 1950–53, as previously discussed, and we will provide you with a cost estimate for this service.' Heck yes I would like those yearbooks. But at eight hundred each, I settled for 1953, senior year." With an accompanying little dance move, he flung back a green plush cover and turned through glossy pages with his pinky raised—"Here's an interesting face. This gal is now fifty-five years old and has a restraining order out against me."

A glance and you knew it was a school yearbook, an-

other glance and you could tell these were high school
Americans after World War II. Ahearn placed a finger beside a face: a charming young woman of the 1950s. A
partial smile, a tilted gaze, perfect curls, the scarf and
rollers probably just removed in the Girls' Room. Only the
black and white head shot, but I could imagine the brown
and white saddle shoes, the ankle-length bobby sox, the
pleated skirt covering her leg to just below the knee. The
tentative smile would indicate a history of braces, but she
was coming out of that now, and better than she realized.
She wore what they called a peasant blouse, a sleeveless
cotton pullover with an elastic neckline that could be low-
ered, when Mom and Dad weren't around, to expose the
shoulders and show a bit of cleavage while vamping with
a cigarette or sipping soda through a straw. The image
struck me hard, knocked me right back to age seven. I
remembered spying and eavesdropping on these very boys
and girls and thinking them the most sophisticated people
in the world.

Alice Mildred Tate

Drama Club

Science Club

Band

Steady Beau: Buck Restell

"Mark. A restraining order?"

"I just want to ask her one question: Does she know

what happened to Buck Restell after 1958? If she says sure, I had coffee with him yesterday—well. Game over."

He flipped the pages in a chunk that fell open to a well-visited site. "Do you see him, Watson?"

"For goodness' sake. Yes." On the left page, top row:

Anthony 'Buck' Restell

Chorus

Drama Club

Steady Beau: Alice Tate

"That is Elvis Presley's twin brother."

~~~~~

Anthony "Buck" Rogers Restell did look like the young Elvis Presley, but plumper in the face, and with a "flat-top" haircut. Ahearn flipped to a later page, a collage of candid snapshots—sports, dances, life between classrooms. A photo of Buck and Alice together in a slow-dance clinch, captioned: *Swept Off Her Feet.*

No photo of the Midwife Sarah Restell among Ahearn's plunder, just one possible image: an old ad on yellow newsprint showing a woman's silhouetted profile—*Madame Restell's Sensitive Salve—The Secret of this Midwife's Success.* "If that's Sarah Jane Restell, then it's all we get to see of her," Mark said. Tenderly he touched the silhouetted nose. "This woman's son, Buck, started out as the baby Jesse Presley."

"Let me understand this. She attended the birth, and stole the baby?"

"She bought the baby. She and the parents bartered with the souls of the twin babes. To the infant Elvis is given worldly success. To the witch is given the infant Jesse to raise as her own child. I won't try and imagine for you the putrid ceremony. Don't scoff, Kev—you know how ghastly superstitious they are down there. Don't you descend from Confederate generals?"

"My mother's from the Smoky Mountains, if that's what you mean. She wasn't a general."

"But you know, Kev, you *know* you know—hoodoo, and rootwork, and the reading of entrails. Down there in the Old Smokies they're cutting dead animals down the middle and casting hexes all the time. Or anyway those superstitions still held tightly to the minds, let us say, in 1935. Do you doubt it? No. So it's a deal—give up one son, see the other shine in life. The bargain's struck, the spell is cast, and the Principalities and Powers take control.

"Years pass . . .

"The twin: What was he like? Flabby, soft. Oozy. Fat, lazy, perverted—infantile appetites, chocolate éclairs, dirty magazines. His favorite music? Dean Martin, or no, somebody less devious and not so much fun: Vic Damone, Perry Como, Bing Crosby. Like Crosby in his youth, Buck sang in the church choir . . . His fake mother thinks he may have been seduced by the choirmaster . . . His mom never married. She wears a wedding ring and styles herself a widow.

"Yes, Sarah Jane Restell received from the Powers exactly what she bargained for—a son to love and raise. Exactly what was promised—and not a morsel beyond that.

"Restell watches her stolen son's twin brother Elvis blaze up in the heavens and streak across the firmament, and his light flickers on the wet of her eyes." (Mark really talked like this—he couldn't help himself; I told you he was a poet.) "In the short space of a couple dozen months the treasures of the earth open themselves for young Elvis, also the hearts of the young multitudes. Restell is choking with envy. The bargain she made seems a mockery, a lie. This is the complex, symphonic Lucifer she's compacted with, the Miltonian genius with the aching, beautiful soul, and it torments Restell how the fallen Son of Light empties himself into this boy Elvis, her son's own twin, and speaks to the fallen world through Elvis's nuanced female gaze and Elvis's jungle-cry music. Restell schemes on a way for her son Buck to participate—maybe as some kind of double for photo shoots or parades. She approaches Colonel Parker with this notion, making him aware of Anthony "Buck" Rogers Restell, a talented Memphis boy who looks the double of young Elvis . . . and of course the debauched colonel smells victims, power, advantage—and things proceed with this conspiracy as with all of poor Lucifer's conspiracies:

Suspicions poison him, he plots against himself, he dispatches demon against demon, and the pact explodes. What follows is bloody murder.

"Parker wanted the hoodlum singer to change his clothes and his music and grow soft and have wider appeal—and pull in more dough. When the army draft came along, Parker saw a chance to murder the rebel Elvis and substitute the docile twin. Parker didn't blink. He pounced, and it was done. As to precisely how the murder of Elvis Presley was accomplished—I won't commit the sacrilege of trying to imagine.

"The army would serve as Parker's magic curtain. The real Elvis disappears behind it. A minimum of publicity during Elvis's military tenure, and then the genius-killer sweeps aside the curtain. There stands the new, domesticated Elvis, with the change accounted for by two years out of the spotlight."

And difference there was, going by this 1953 yearbook image of Buck, or Jesse—a remarkable resemblance around the eyes, and yet they didn't smolder, and the lips were shaped identically, though not the mouth, not the expression, no Elvis sneer. The jawline, yes, the chin almost exactly Elvis's, but the flesh beneath the chin too fatty, self-indulgent, sculpted from those éclairs. Each component quite close, but the whole, like a composite police sketch, somehow bearing no genuine resemblance. "Jesse could sing and dance, and while he didn't have the deep relationship with the camera that Elvis had, he could emote in a camera's presence, and he did as directed by the directors, and obeyed the colonel, and enjoyed, or endured, a career.

"On a worldly level, Parker had a strong motive for murder, maybe an irresistible one for a greedy man. But Parker's real motive was occult. He wanted to assert his identity as Evil's prefect, Evil's provincial mayor, and his province was the Province of Mediocrity. I hope I can suggest this, Kev, without turning your stomach: The murder of Elvis Presley had a sacrificial element."

Three months prior to his enlistment, the actual Elvis allowed his sideburns "to be taken," was Ahearn's phrasing, "probably as a sign of surrender, or, let's state it plainly, a symbolic castration before the evil father figure, Colonel Parker. But Parker didn't feel truly *fed*, not till he'd devoured Elvis's life itself." As Mark spoke, his fingertips wandered over his documents, touching and greeting them, the scrolls and relics of a private worship. Here was a man completely sane in almost any respect, but on this table he'd arranged meaningless papers and books that had set him back thousands. If the forgers and con artists hadn't found him, it seemed only a matter of time. Not that Mark looked easy to fool. He had these wonderfully patrician rippling-caterpillar eyebrows, rectangular beasts with highlights of red and blond, bearing down on you—did I mention his auburn hair? And if I called his eyes pale blue, perhaps I should have said gray. His eyes themselves seemed to throb in their sockets. I didn't feel like contradicting him.

"This is Jesse Garon Presley, the twin of Elvis Presley; not stillborn; born alive beside the future King of Rock 'n' Roll, stolen by the sorceress midwife Sarah Jane Restell, who recorded a false death certificate and raised him as her own son for seventeen years and then turned him over to the diabolist Tom Parker, who in turn exploited poor Jesse for twenty years, until Jesse died on the toilet and was placed in the tomb of his brother, Elvis, himself already perished, murdered, and his corpse destroyed, no doubt, never to be restored to his family, or to the millions who felt a kinship.

"Can I tell you something sad?

"Sarah Jane Restell had no family in the world but Jesse. She brought him near the colonel, and in 1958 Jesse vanished into the army as into a black hole in space. No communication with her son, her only family, except through the colonel. And then, on August 11th, 1958, the spellbinder Sarah Jane Restell dies in circumstances never questioned, never given any light—I say probably poisoned, probably by the colonel—but let it go.

"Madame Restell died alone.

"Jesse (now Private Elvis Presley) learned, through his

master the colonel, of his adopted mother's death and went
into shock and grief in Fort Hood, Texas, surrounded by his
comrades in Company A of the Third Armored Division's
1st Medium Tank Battalion. But he couldn't explain his
upset, except to say, 'My Mom, my Mom . . .' When brought
the news that his birth mother, Gladys, whom he never
knew or cared about, was dying at Graceland, Jesse was
delivered a credible excuse for the misery that everyone
could see was overwhelming him.

"Jesse wasn't permitted to honor or mourn his beloved
Sarah publicly. He could howl all he wanted, as long as he
howled for Gladys. The army granted him leave to attend
Gladys's last hours and her service. At the funeral he
howled, all right, he blubbered, he even fainted several
times before, during, and after the ceremony—all for Sarah
Jane Restell. On the same day, Madame Restell was buried
without a service or any mourners at the Pike Hill Cemetery outside Memphis, but her grave is no longer there.
Estes, Franks tell me Sarah Restell was disinterred at the
request of relatives—she had none—and moved to an unknown location." Ahearn glows like a distant fire, Edgar
Poe possesses him: "Sarah Restell was moved, I say, to a
sub-basement many leagues beneath the Graceland Mansion. A spiral staircase, a hidden vault, a place for Jesse's
corrosive, solitary grief, and the source of an addicting pu-
trescence, the love of the devil-mother, and she fed on her

son until he died on the floor of the bathroom two stories above her vault. Her son of two names, Jesse Garon and Elvis Aaron. Her doppelgänger son."

~~~~~~

Dreams He Eats, Marcus Ahearn's fourth book, came out in the spring of 2001. Scattered through its forty-three poems I found five brief, good-humored pieces depicting day-to-day moments in the life of a professor called Somers Garfield. But it was me. Somers Garfield was Kevin Harrington.

Professor Garfield, for instance, drops coins into a panhandler's fresh cup of coffee—I recalled the incident, but I saw nothing personal in its use. Then I read about myself erupting in the classroom, once again looking foolish in words that will never die. Twelve pages later I'm ordering a sandwich at a deli counter and falling into the Abyss, the one I thought I'd kept hidden. Does it mean I'm childish, or ungenerous, that I felt several different ways, but mainly resentful, felt exploited, violated, when I saw myself walking around half-naked in somebody else's creations?—so I asked in a long, handwritten letter, one of a multitude Mark never received. Nothing on paper would communicate the tone of the query—wounded, yes, but also academically interested in whether I have a right to feel that way . . . I had to ask him face to face: Am I Somers Garfield?

Of course, between our Slocum Pond meeting in '91 and

Dreams He Eats in 2001, Mark and I crossed paths a few times. And we talked on the phone every three or four months. Elvis always came up as a topic—never Somers Garfield. Somers Garfield could wait until the autumn, at the retirement celebration of Mark's long-time editor, Edison Steptoe. I had no other reason to go to New York, or anywhere else for that matter—really, I couldn't claim to be anywhere. The bare facts: Anne and I divorced and sold the Wellfleet house, and Anne moved to Spain. I joined the English Department at a pretty good college in central Illinois which I won't name because I was so very unhappy there through no fault of theirs. I wandered, or trudged, through a colorless, leafless, damp winter's day that never changed, whether June came, or April or August, no matter, it never changed. In time I dropped my poet's persona; since then I've masqueraded as a literary critic, and with a great deal more success, but criticism isn't real—it's not a real thing. So excelling at it hasn't healed me. In trying to get this Somers Garfield business squared away with Mark Ahearn, I might have been seeking a healing. I got myself invited to Steptoe's celebration and hopped a flight.

These events can be really second-rate, but not this one—I gave the planners high marks. In a tall midtown building, eighty or so well-wishers eased amongst each other downing canapés and free liquor in the vicinity of ten big tables arranged for the farewell feast. The access to alcohol and the prospect of more food set everyone aglow. Today happened to be, as I knew, Mark Ahearn's forty-second birthday, but I'm not sure Mark himself remembered. I'd last seen him in '97. After four years, in addition to looking heavier, with a heavier gait, he seemed distracted, a prisoner of his thoughts in the midst of frolic, and I believe he was avoiding his editor and mentor, Edison Steptoe, who made a speech and was given a plaque and then toured the room holding the plaque in the crook of his arm, filling the premises with his big, onrushing face, his bush of brown hair floating above his head and following it around. I never liked him. I admired his deeds. I approved especially of his steady support of Marcus Ahearn. Under his own imprint, Steptoe had built a daunting list of poets from all over the Americas, and Mark was the one he kept most prominent. But the charismatic editor always had around him this contingent of darling, curly-haired young women and slender-fingered young men, all poets. They made me nervous.

Steptoe and I had a moment alone. Fresh drinks and re-introductions on a balcony fourteen floors above Fifth Avenue—almost night. In the purple sky, four or five stars crowned the Empire State Building. The others, the editor's elfin admirers, his bodyguard of Peter Pans and Orphan Annies, started talking about that. I had a chance to consult with him about a matter that had come up between me and Mark recently—more documents out of Tupelo and Memphis—Mark's latest and greatest expenditure. It wasn't my money, but I worried anyway. Steptoe could lend an ear, maybe a voice—frankly, I hoped he'd stick his nose in. "The latest document is a single page torn from the personal diary of Elvis's birth doctor. Mark tells me he paid eighty-five hundred bucks."

Steptoe, a tall man, peered down at me, all smiles, witless. "Elvis Presley's diary?"

"No. His doctor's diary, and only one page of it. And then, to verify the thing, his law firm charges a nice fat fee. And as long as Mark's willing to pay like that—well, the world's always got something to sell, right?"

Watching Steptoe's face as he gathered in these words and plainly comprehended none of them, I felt my stomach plunge . . . Inadvertently I'd snitched my friend Mark. I measured the balcony's railing with the thought of hopping over. It seemed the quickest exit. Here's what you say when you screw up like this: "I might be mixing up two or three subjects. I'll shut up."

Others dragged Steptoe away—but the incident told me that Mark was hiding from his long-time mentor a passion that had, in many respects, overmastered his life. Had he made me his sole confessor?

At that moment, Ahearn stepped onto the balcony and gripped my arm. He'd celebrated enough—he hated crowds,

I remembered that now. We could smell the free, catered dinner, but Mark wanted to go. "I chose the medallions of sirloin," I told him. He hustled me out past friendly faces, through a song of friendly voices—"Well done!" and "Congratulations!"—*Dreams He Eats* had been nominated for a National Book Award. Mark steered me by my elbow out of the building and down through the pungent streets on this night too warm for his flapping Dylan-Thomas trench coat.

Mark had a place in mind two blocks west, Italian aromas, candles flickering all around, almost like a bomb shelter, I thought. He paused to read the menu mounted just inside. The face turned toward its little light seemed sad, even old.

No pity. I was prepared to drill him with four ridiculous-sounding words: Am I Somers Garfield?

But even before we sat down, he rifled his overcoat and slapped a flat manila envelope on the table. "I shouldn't be giving you this."

"Then don't."

"This is the page from Dr. Hunt's journal. This is what really happened the night Elvis Presley was born. It completely contradicts the entry in this same doctor's 'baby book.' Which, incidentally, was a CIA put-up job."

"Oh, Lord."

"This is a photocopy. The original's in my safe. The legal

geniuses Estes and Franks," he said, "have warned me I shouldn't have it. It was stolen in a burglary. I couldn't tell you that over the phone."

"I mean, eighty-five hundred. God, Mark."

"Lotta dough. And to verify the origin of this one piece of paper, old Estes tagged me for two thousand more."

"It's verified?"

"Partly, mostly—sufficiently. Their cover letter's stapled to it."

"Mark, when I hear the letters C, and I, and A—"

"I'll give this to you now. Take it. Tomorrow we'll talk. Take it, Kev!—it's not booby-trapped."

We settled down to a Chianti-fest. Not a happy one.

I might have seen Mark drunk once or twice. But not drunk and defeated. Apparently he'd expended more than money trying to get the state of Mississippi to exhume the grave of the infant Jesse Garon Presley. He'd burned up his fuel, his hope. "No amount of evidence will satisfy the fools. And they say I don't have a legal claim of injury—no dog in the fight, they say, and I'm the only one who wants a fight anyway." Later, drunker, he said, "But I could get more evidence. I'll exhume the grave myself." And a little later he said, "Imagine a child's coffin dragged up after sixty-plus years in the cold, moldy ground, dangling roots and clots and dripping putrefaction." (Somebody at another table wondered, "Do people really have to talk so *loud*?")

Around midnight, I put him in a cab. We agreed on lunch the next day, but not on where. Mark's mood seemed lighter.

He went his way to friends on the upper west side, and I went mine, tipsy, hyperventilating the late summer oxygen. During a brief subway ride I ripped open Ahearn's envelope and squinted at a photocopied page. ". . . A preponderance of facts would support a claim to authenticity (See Exhibits A–H). However, let it be noted that some facts would serve to undermine, if not refute, the claim (See Exhibits I–L) . . ." I rolled up and folded the pages as tightly as I could, as if to compress this entire affair into a state of non-existence, climbed up into the city, and soon dumped my boozy head on a pillow at my digs—the Chelsea on West Twenty-Third downtown, an 1800s-built tomb of moaning wooden bones, tilted, hazardous, trading on its long bohemian legacy only to make it the excuse for slow ruin. No restaurant. No room service. Abandon your assumptions about elevators. "There are no vacuum cleaners, no rules, and no shame," said Arthur Miller, who nevertheless lived several years under its roof. I stayed there for the art, the walls laid over from floor to ceiling with paintings, the bold sculptures guarding all the nooks and crannies, the hordes of beatnik-era mobiles dropping from the ceilings like an airborne division. Anybody could turn up at the Chelsea—the next morning, for instance, I stepped into the small doubtful elevator by myself, and on the fourth floor I picked up the actor Peter O'Toole. In the shock of finding us shut up together and breathing each other's breath, I told him, "I think you're a great person. *The Ruling Class, Lawrence of Arabia*"—and so on, and Peter O'Toole listened to me closely, in happy surprise, as if he'd never heard of these movies before, or even of himself. In the middle of the kooky, art-bound lobby he stopped for an elderly couple who wanted to tell him exactly the same thing, and for almost a minute he gave them his full, sincere, smiling attention—his eyes, by the way, were actually that blue. At the moment, I was heading anywhere at all for breakfast, but when I heard the desk clerk's radio playing news that an aircraft, I assumed a sightseeing plane, had struck Tower Two of the World Trade Center, I decided to jump on the number 3 subway half a block west, and go have a look.

As I headed toward Eighth Avenue I tried calling Mark Ahearn about lunch, but my cellphone only hammered out a rapid-fire beep. Please don't ask me how this can be true: I traveled through the busy lobby and walked for half a long block on a crowded Manhattan street and then boarded the World Trade Center subway completely unaware that I was participating in a citywide disaster, and moving toward its center.

The World Trade Center station came a few stops south of Twenty-Third Street, but we didn't get there. After Christopher Street the train halted in the tunnel and waited, humming. It gave a screech, lurched backward slightly, and stopped again. Somehow the general news had infiltrated the sealed subterranean environment that something historically enormous was happening very nearby, and it got quiet in our compartment, and almost everybody entered into a small, desperate battle with a worthless cellphone. The train moved forward and gained speed, but began braking long before Houston Street, the next station, where it halted with several rear cars sticking out behind into the tunnel. For a tense minute, whoever spoke only whispered. Then came a shout—"Tell us what's going on!" and others raised the same cry until we heard the conductor's PA saying something about the tracks, the tracks . . . "Due to the catastrophe, this train will not go farther. Please exit out the forward cars onto the platform. Do not go onto the tracks." We were all on our feet, maneuvering selfishly, angling for the doors. But the doors didn't open. The engine stopped. "Open the doors! Open the doors!" The engine started. A man shouted, "Just everybody stand still!" People from the car behind had pried their way into ours, and somebody almost went down. A woman said, "Stop that, you fool!" A man in front of me pushed a teenage boy beside him. With the meat of his fist he began beating the back of the boy's head. And I jumped into the fray, didn't you, Harrington, like a monkey, yes you did, and got yourself an elbow in the eye. The doors to the compartment flew open and people clambered out onto the station's platform, where a dreadlocked man in a crimson athletic suit jumped up and down on a bench as if it were a trampoline, screaming *"God, see what we're doing to each other down here."* When I came up into the street, dizzy and one-eyed, I couldn't get my bearings. I saw only one tower standing to the south, and that one ringed with fire. I asked a man nearby—"Where are we? I can't see the other tower." He said, "It fell," and I said, "No it didn't." He didn't argue. We stood in the middle of the street with thousands of other people, all of us motionless, like a frozen parade, all silent. I began to believe the man. We watched the flames spreading through the building's upper stories over the course of about twenty minutes, and then the eighteen-hundred-foot structure seemed to curtsy and dip left, and then it went down.

I turned around and looked at the people behind me. I saw shocked laughter, weeping, horror, bewilderment. The young man next to me bawled at the top of his lungs. I was afraid to ask him if he had a loved one in the buildings— afraid to talk to him at all, but he raised his agonized, Christly face to me and suddenly laughed, saying, "Buddy, you are working on one heck of a black eye." We stood far from the buildings—at least a mile, I'd say—far enough that we didn't feel the ground shake, and we heard nothing but sirens, and official-sounding voices screaming,

"Get out of the street! Stay out of the street!" and others too—"They're attacking the Capitol!—the Pentagon!—the White House!"

Cop cars and ambulances heaped with dust and chunks of concrete came at us out of the south. I started walking that direction, I don't know why, but I soon realized I was the only person heading downtown, and then the tide of panic pressing toward me was too heavy to go against, and I turned around and let it take me north.

I'd forgotten about my date with Mark, and years later he assured me he'd forgotten it too.

~~~~~

I wondered if Mark Ahearn wasn't making his debut as a public fanatic when he interrupted a reading of his work with the opening bars to "Love Me," a number from Elvis's self-titled 1956 album—

> *Treat me like a fool,*
> *Treat me mean and cruel,*
> *But love me . . .*

—to the mystified delight of the audience at the National Book Awards ceremony. *Dreams He Eats* didn't win, but they made him read from it anyway.

The following January 8—now 2002—my phone buzzed

quite early. I guessed it was Mark, because it was Elvis's sixty-seventh birthday, but too early on Elvis's sixty-seventh birthday for anything approaching civilized exchange, so I let it go to voice mail, and an hour later I picked up this message:

"I'm calling from the motel. I'm in Tupelo, Kev. I just came from the graveyard, just walked through the door. I'm getting dirt all over the phone"—noises, fumbling, wiping—"I opened the coffin, Kev. There's a little corpse in there, and I looked into its face."

I left a voice mail in exchange. I didn't hear back, and kept calling. After a couple of weeks Mark poked his head out of hiding and we talked, but only on the phone. He refused to acknowledge his first message to me—"I just came from the graveyard," et cetera. Cagey, mysterious, legal—"Don't forget my friends Estes and Franks. They're my friends too, the same as you, and I'm heeding their advice to shut up." I devised a question he could answer without incriminating himself: "Are you satisfied, these days, as to the contents of Jesse Presley's grave?" He said yes; he believed the grave covered a coffin, and the coffin held a baby. Then he went farther, too far: "All right, goddamn it, sure, I dug it up. It's a deep, dark crime, and it's on my soul. But you've read the doctor's report, the account in his journal. What else could I do? The doctor left me no choice." He broke the connection.

Since the night of 9/11, I hadn't given a thought to Mark's eighty-five-hundred-dollar piece of paper, but I knew where to find it. In my bathrobe and long johns and unlaced boots, I stumbled through dirty snow out to my garage, a wooden shed attached to the farmhouse I rented there in Illinois. In my car I found my travel bag, and in a pocket in the bag, like trash, like lint, the powering motive for Mark's spiritual felony.

You step into that kind of January, the midwestern kind, in the last light around 5 p.m., a faded, frozen pink light originating along the horizon, and you don't get warm again soon. In the house I turned up the heat and placed a dining chair over the floor grate. I sat down, tore away the cover letter, and read:

Jan. 8, 1935
Jessie [*sic*] Garon Presley b. 4:00 AM dec'd. ?
Evis [*sic*] Aaron Presley b. 4:35 AM

Summoned by telephone to Presley residence N. Saltillo Rd. by a neighbor Mrs. A. Thompson, who said she heard the screams of the birthing.

Arrived 4:15 AM, and a midwife who opened door to me said, I will bury the boy born dead, and went immediately into the night with a stillbirth bundled in a pillowcase.

Found mother Gladys Presley abed, father Vernon
Presley in kitchen. The young husband appeared drunk.
His only words to me were these—"We never called on you
to come, Sir."

I want to note the way of their behaving in the circumstance, as follows: There was no joy at the birth of the live
one. No sorrow at the death of the first-born. As soon as
the second boy came forth without complication, mother
asked me to leave. When I referred to $15 fee, the hus-
band repeated he did not call me, the neighbor called me.

I felt most uneasy and none of this set right with me,
foremost, the midwife's departure with the stillborn. I said
I could not file a death certificate. They said it would be
filed. Citing the law, I demanded the midwife's particulars
and was given the name Sarah Jane Restell.

First making sure of the newborn's vitals, I ended this
visit.

~~~~~

Yes. Mark plundered an infant's grave. If he'd told me in
advance, if he'd asked me to come along, to abet him, serve
as his accomplice, would I have agreed? Instantly. Grate-
fully. I discount his theory, but I value the obsession. And I
commend his nerve. Old southern graveyards harbor an
unwholesome power comparable to that of nuclear disaster
sites. My mother's people came, as I think I've indicated,

from the Carolinas; everybody down there knows that the graves at night tremble underfoot, if anyone were crazy or curious enough to walk on them under a waning crescent moon, and this is what Marcus Ahearn was doing that night in the Priceville Cemetery outside Tupelo with a shrouded flashlight, manhandling the graves, looking for a metal marker numbered "867" buried beneath the winter grass. Besides the flashlight he carried a pick and a spade, wore work gloves and work boots and Carhartt overalls, all newly purchased at Tupelo's Sears outlet, that much I eventually learned. And Mark knew how to dig in the dirt—his old job as a landscaper—descending a little better than two feet per hour; if he started at midnight, he was brushing the rot from the coffin by 3 a.m. And soon after that was staring into the face, if face there remained, of a sixty-seven-year-old baby.

Mark remained coy about the details. I presume he replaced the coffin in its hole and covered it up again. Ersatz corpses, ersatz documents, false trails, furious complications. I waited to see how he'd make sense of it all. I waited for years.

My father died. Mark's mother died. My mother died. Mark's father died. As soon as he was orphaned, Mark dove deep into women: six years, three marriages. And me? No. I won't marry again. Pity me—I'm still in love with Anne.

In recent years my contact with Mark, though infrequent, has been warm, and nothing forces us to stay in touch. We'll always be friends. But it has to be said that Mark and I have gone our separate ways.

Another fact: Mark's last book was *Dreams He Eats* in 2001, fifteen years ago.

~~~~~~

Six years ago, in the springtime, I traveled to Portland University to give a talk on the Black Mountain poets. Nobody came. At the appointed hour a student led me from the English Department offices to a chemistry auditorium and left me to myself, and in five more minutes a fast-moving, bow-tied Lecturer in English wheeled in a cart bearing canapés and coffee and juice, introduced me to the microphone, handed me a check for a few hundred dollars, and explained to me in a delighted whisper in the silent, empty auditorium that the person in charge of the speakers' program, a Ms. Charlene Kennedy, had experienced a personal, psychological breakdown of a possibly romantic nature and run away to Portugal, leaving the program's affairs a ball of confusion, particularly as regarded our little visit—my visit, here and now—for which no publicity had been arranged. That I waited here with a microphone, a podium, and snacks for eighty people was a deeply buried secret. After presenting me with my fee, my host shook my hand and assured me nobody expected me to hang around and pretend to earn it, and apologized for the additional circumstance that he, himself, had to leave immediately for a departmental get-together. Ms. Charlene Kennedy, wherever you are, I wave my middle finger at you. It makes for kind of a funny story now, but at the time I felt stupid and unlucky.

But Mark Ahearn turned up.

His hair was long and tangled, he was unshaven, he wore a big sweater, his shoes were old. I took in these impressions as he made his way toward me without pausing but with the air, absolutely, of somebody who thought he'd found the wrong room, rotating slowly even as he stepped along, reconnoitering, searching for anybody else, I supposed.

"There's nobody else," I told him.

He took me in his embrace. Loudly and somewhat wetly he kissed my cheek. He'd aged. Gray-headed, wrinkles deep as scars on his cheeks. The whites of his eyes were red, the irises blue, the whole effect was purple. I'd heard rumors he had bouts of—something. Drink, or powders, or accelerated mania and depression . . . Marcus Ahearn hadn't produced a book in the last nine years.

All the same, his eyes held humor and fire. "I haven't seen you since the death of the Twins."

"What twins? Oh, yes, oh—you mean the Twin Towers." Twin Towers, twin Presleys, twin Ahearns. The pairings of these pairs must have beaten on his thoughts with considerable intensity. It hadn't even occurred to me.

Mark and I sat side by side on the apron of the stage, feet dangling, and tried the sandwich triangles. Along the wall to our left, a chart depicting the Periodic Table. On the right, just outside a high run of windows, masses of evergreens tinted by the sunset. Behind us a pair of comfortable chairs flanked the podium, waiting for an on-stage interview, a part of the day's agenda I hadn't known about. Mark now revealed himself to be my moderator, or partner, for this discussion. (Had Ms. Charlene Kennedy completed her tasks, this information would have reached me.) Mark taught at the U of Oregon in Eugene, two hours' drive from Portland, and he'd been there for years. "Since I stopped publishing, they think I'm one of them. They're trying to give me tenure. But it's hard, Kev. They want you to act like you want it."

I wanted tenure at my midwestern college. That was the height and the depth of me. However—"Mark."

"Kev."

"The Elvis thing . . . Have you ever mentioned it to anybody else?"

"No."

"Your wives?"

"Oh, no. Even by the time Miss Huntley came along, that phase was already over. She was the first wife."

"That phase."

"The whole Elvis conspiracy phase. It was deep, Kev,
but it wasn't endless."

"I'm the only one who knew."

"In all this time. Yes."

"Why make me your confessor?"

I'm sure I saw the truth coming, the truth was there in
his face, and then I'm sure it went away—untold—and his
face told this lie instead:

"Why you? Because you understand what it is to be
moved by Elvis Presley. I know that's a stupid-sounding
thing to say. But you understand, and that's a fact I'm sure
of. And there's something else: You're frail, Kev, you have
this quality—as if your childhood terrors aren't done with
you."

"That sounds like the thing you wish was the reason—
but it isn't. You're covering up."

"What am I covering up?"

"Mark, I'm your closest reader on this earth. I know
when you're lying and when you're telling the truth. You
almost always tell the truth."

Silence. He set aside his triangular sandwich, working
his lips as if tasting the thing he wasn't saying. He looked at
the wall running left of us, studying the display of the Periodic Table, the elemental categories of material existence
and the symbols for them, not moving his eyes, I noticed,

although if he had a particular element in focus, I couldn't tell which one, and I thought, For goodness' sake. He's stuck for words.

"I wanted Lance's epitaph to say, 'The gods worshipped him.' My parents said it would shock."

"And what is his epitaph?"

"We never chose one. Not for his twin either. Did I tell you my brothers are buried side by side? Five feet and eighteen years apart."

"No epitaphs."

"Just the name of each. Lancaster Smith Ahearn . . ."

"And the other?"

"Somers Garfield."

I think I displayed my shock in an exaggerated way, eyes and mouth widening to swallow the rest of my face while I jumped straight up into the air, like a street mime.

Mark laughed. "You recognize the name! How come you never asked me, 'What's this between your old Professor Harrington and Somers Garfield?' Do you know how long I've been waiting for you to ask that question?"

As coldly as I could, I said, "Screw the question, Mark. What is the *answer*?"

"Kevin Peter Harrington: You are the reincarnation of Somers Garfield Ahearn, my brother's stillborn twin."

"I'm your brother."

"Somers was born and died on July thirteenth, 1949.

You came into the world one week later, am I right? July twenty, 1949?"

An automatic laugh and a ten-pound lump in the stomach, that's how I'd expect to respond to this presumptuous loony assault on my spiritual person. But, no, in this case I felt charmed. Marcus Ahearn and I, named brothers by the planets themselves and the stellar influences—whoever decides these things. I felt liberated by this crazy, silly little scene in the empty auditorium with the Periodic Table to the side. I noticed many elements I'd never heard of—brand new elements, and I felt one myself, flashing forth from the quantum soup, sprung from uncertainty itself. "I'm your brother." I believe it to this day.

~~~~~

When he was my student, I told Marcus Ahearn he wrote wonderfully. He said it wasn't the most important thing he did.

I wonder if that isn't the secret of his greatness. I wonder if his mania doesn't ease the pressure of his genius and make it bearable.

Our country's finest poet, Marcus Ahearn, hasn't published a poem in fifteen years, not a single line of verse. Two days ago, on Elvis's birthday, the Memphis police arrested him at Graceland. I wouldn't be surprised if the waking of the Elvis beast coincided with a creative burst, another re-markable book.

Two months ago I got an email from Mark Ahearn in which he picked up a very old thread: *The timeshare story—remember the Brights, Ron and Opal? The chronology there would indicate that in November, 1958, Elvis was already a ghost. He stated that he'd been walking the streets of Paradise—deceased. In 1958.*

I answered instantly, pointing out that in order to accept this proof that Elvis was in Paradise in 1958, we first have to accept life after death, Paradise, ghosts, all of that.

Mark answered a couple of days later, *I smile and shrug. Life after death, ghosts, Paradise, eternity—of course, we take all that as granted. Otherwise where's the fun?*

He closed the first message—*Peace/Love/Elvis.* The second—

Elvisly Yours.

ABOUT THE AUTHOR

Denis Johnson was the author of nine novels, one novella, two books of short stories, five collections of poetry, two collections of plays, and one book of reportage. Among other honors, his novel *Tree of Smoke* won the 2007 National Book Award and was a finalist for the 2008 Pulitzer Prize, and *Train Dreams* was a finalist for the 2012 Pulitzer Prize.

ABOUT THE TYPE

This book was set in Bodoni Book, a typeface named after Giambattista Bodoni (1740–1813), an Italian printer and type designer. It is not actually one of Bodoni's fonts but a modern version based on his style and manner and is distinguished by a marked contrast between the thick and thin elements of the letters.